LOVE IN SUMMER CAMP

VEBSTER AGMEY JR.

Made with ♥ on the Notion Press Platform
www.notionpress.com

To my daughter, Veronica

"The day you were born was the most beautiful day of my life. From that moment on, you became my world, my greatest joy, and my reason to keep going. Every smile of yours is a blessing, every moment with you is a gift.

This book is for you, my little star. May you always dream big, love fearlessly, and create your own beautiful story in life."

With all my love,

Daddy

Contents

Foreword   *vii*

Preface   *ix*

Acknowledgements   *xi*

Prologue   *xiii*

1. Chapter 1   1

2. Chapter 2   11

3. Chapter 3   20

4. Chapter 4   27

5. Chapter 5   33

6. Chapter 6   40

7. Chapter 7   45

8. Chapter 8   53

9. Chapter 9   61

10. Chapter 10   65

11. Chapter 11   78

12. Chapter 12   86

13. Chapter 13   99

14. Chapter 14   106

15. Chapter 15   115

16. Chapter 16   132

Foreword

"*Every love story is unique, but some leave a lasting imprint on our hearts, this is one of them. Love in Summer Camp is not just a novel; it is a journey through time, emotions, and memories that refuse to fade.*

This story was born from a deep belief in the magic of first love, the nostalgia of youthful days, and the way life brings people together when they least expect it. Through the pages of this book, I invite you to step into a world where summer romances feel eternal, where the ocean carries whispers of the past, and where love is tested by fate itself.

I hope this book takes you on a journey of emotions, of laughter, longing, and the beauty of love that never truly leaves us."

Preface

"Some dreams take years to come true. Some stories live within us, growing, evolving, waiting for the right moment to be told. Love in Summer Camp is one such story, one that stayed in my heart for over a decade, whispering to me, urging me to put it into words.

I am not a professional writer; I am a banker by profession. But before I was a writer, I was a dreamer, a reader, and a hopeless romantic at heart. My love for stories began in 2008 when I first picked up a book. I read everything I could get my hands on, romantic stories, historical tales, even the Ramayana and the Bible. Reading wasn't just a hobby; it became my passion, my escape, my way of living different lives within the pages of a book.

But books were not my only inspiration. I grew up watching Bollywood romantic movies, the kind where love conquers all, where emotions run high, where a single glance can say a thousand words. And above all, I was a big fan of Shah Rukh Khan, the man who defined romance for an entire generation. His movies made me believe in love, in destiny, in stories that touch the heart. Somewhere deep inside, a thought started forming, what if I could create a love story of my own?

For the past ten years, Love in Summer Camp has lived within me. I have written and rewritten it at least fifty to sixty times. Every version felt like a rehearsal, a rough draft of the perfect love story

I wanted to bring to life. There were moments of frustration, times when I thought I would never get it right. But like love itself, a true story refuses to fade away. It lingers, it grows stronger, and then, one day, it finds its perfect form.

This book is not just a novel; it's a part of my soul, a piece of my journey, a reflection of the love stories I have admired and dreamed of. It is about love, longing, fate, and the magic of finding someone who makes your heart race.

So, here it is. My story. My dream. I hope it makes you feel something, just as it made me feel everything while writing it."

Acknowledgements

"Writing Love in Summer Camp has been a journey of passion, dedication, and inspiration. I would like to express my deepest gratitude to those who have played a significant role in shaping my path as a writer.

First and foremost, I extend my heartfelt thanks to my father Prof. N. V. Agmey, awarded poet and gifted writer, whose creativity and dedication to literature have been my greatest source of inspiration. From an early age, I watched him compose poetry, write thought, provoking articles, and captivate audiences at Kavi Sammelans. His unwavering passion for storytelling and the written word has profoundly influenced me, shaping my love for writing and fueling my determination to complete this novel.

I am also immensely grateful to Mr. Sanjay Singh, NSM - Kotak Mahindra Prime Ltd, a great leader and an inspiring influencer. His wisdom, leadership, and ability to motivate those around him have left a lasting impact on my life. I have learned countless invaluable lessons from him, both professionally and personally. His presence in my journey has been significant, and for that, I extend my sincere appreciation.

To all those who have supported, encouraged, and believed in me thank you. This book is a testament to the guidance and inspiration I have *received along the way.*"

Prologue

"*Love has a way of finding us when we least expect it, sometimes in the warmth of a summer breeze, sometimes in the quiet moments of longing.*

It all began in Goa, where a 16-year-old Sunil met a girl Nutan at a summer camp. Beneath the swaying palm trees, by the endless blue sea, he felt something he had never felt before, the thrill of first love. The excitement of stolen glances, the rush of shared laughter, and the promise of forever, even when forever was just a word.

But life is never as simple as a summer romance. Time moves forward, and so did he, away from the beaches of Goa, into the chaotic yet beautiful city of Mumbai. The city that never sleeps, where dreams are born and hearts are tested. Among the towering skyscrapers and crowded streets, memories of that summer still lingered, pushing him toward a journey he never imagined a journey to find the love he once knew.

Was it just a fleeting moment, or was it something more?

This is a story of first love, distance, and the search for something lost yet unforgettable. Because some summers change us forever, and some hearts refuse to forget.

Welcome to Love in Summer Camp...

By - Vebster Agmey Jr."

ONE

May – 2004 Love in Summer Camp

The final Bell

The golden sun shined brightly in the sky, spreading its warmth over the small, quiet town of Verna in Goa. This little town was full of green fields, tall coconut trees, and narrow roads. The air smelled like the sea, mixed with the sweet scent of ripe mangoes. The summer heat was strong, but my heart was beating fast, not because of the heat or the history exam paper in front of me. My mind had already left this classroom, thinking about the fun waiting for me outside.

The exam hall was silent except for the soft sound of pens scratching on paper and the old ceiling fan making a slow, creaking noise. The fan, which had been in the classroom for many years, turned lazily, making a clicking sound like an old man complaining. The room smelled of sweat, ink, and old books.

My pen was in my hand, but my thoughts were far away. History, names, dates, and battles, were written on my paper, but I was not thinking about them. Instead, I was dreaming about the days ahead. Just a few more minutes, and I would be free. I could already imagine myself running through the narrow streets of Verna, feeling the warm air on my face as I rode my bicycle past the coconut trees.

The examiner stood at the front of the room, watching us carefully. He had a thick moustache and wore glasses. His white shirt was neat, and his sleeves were folded up. He had a serious look on his face. He crossed his arms and tapped his fingers against his arm, as if waiting for time to pass. Sometimes, he adjusted his glasses and cleared his throat, making everyone sit up straight.

My fingers tapped on the desk. Sweat ran down my forehead, not because of fear but because of the heat. The window was open, but only warm air and the sound of birds came in. My mind wandered again, two months of holidays were waiting for me. I imagined running on the beach, playing cricket with my friends, and riding my bicycle until I was too tired. The thought was so exciting that I almost forgot about the exam.

A sharp voice brought me back. "Five minutes left!" the examiner said in a loud, deep voice. My heart jumped. Just five more minutes, and I would be free.

The other students were still writing quickly, but I had lost interest. I looked at the clock, watching the second hand move slowly. Each tick was a step closer to my freedom.

Tringgggg!

The final bell rang. The silence in the room broke as students put down their pens, shuffled their papers, and sighed in relief. I quickly handed my answer sheet to the examiner and rushed out of the classroom.

The hallway was full of students talking, laughing, and running towards the exit. I pushed through the crowd, my heart full of excitement. As I stepped outside, the sun hit my face, and I took a deep breath. The air smelled fresh and warm.

Verna looked beautiful. The coconut trees moved gently in the wind. The small streets, with colorful houses and arched windows, felt welcoming. The sound of church bells in the distance reminded me that I was home, in a place where life was slow and peaceful.

I ran to my bicycle, grabbed the handlebars, and got ready for my first ride of the summer. The wind would rush past me, the sun would shine on my face, and I would feel completely free.

Summer had begun, and my adventure was just starting.

The world outside the exam hall felt like a new place. The air was fresh, carrying the scent of blooming flowers and freshly watered fields. The sky stretched wide and clear, as if welcoming me back into its embrace. The streets of Verna, once feeling like endless paths leading to school, now felt open and inviting, ready for new adventures. The moment I stepped out, the burden of exams melted away, and I felt light, free.

I ran towards the cycle stand, where my friends were already waiting. Their faces were lit with excitement, their grins wide. Sandeep threw his arms in the air. "Summer vacation starts now, boys!" he declared.

"No school, no teachers, just fun!" Pawan added, slapping my back.

I jumped onto my cycle, gripping the handlebars with renewed energy. "Cricket at Arossim Beach?" I asked, already knowing the answer.

"Obviously!" Pawan smirked. "Loser buys cold drinks!"

Arossim Beach was about ten kilometers from our school, and it had always been our favorite playground. The soft sand, the cool sea breeze, and the endless space made it perfect for our matches. It was scorching hot, but we didn't care. We pedaled with all our might, a group of carefree boys racing through the streets of Verna, our laughter echoing as the warm wind brushed against our faces.

The roads stretched before us, lined with tall palm trees swaying lazily under the bright sun. Small houses with red-tiled roofs and vibrant flower gardens passed by in a blur. The scent of the sea grew stronger with each pedal, mixing with the distant aroma of street food being prepared at roadside stalls.

We raced through the narrow lanes, dodging potholes, waving at familiar faces, and teasing each other along the way. A group of fishermen walked past, carrying baskets filled with their fresh catch of the day, their voices rising in cheerful conversation. We passed by a small bakery, the smell of freshly baked poi (Goan bread) making our mouths water.

"Let's grab a snack before we get there!" Vikram called out, slowing his cycle near the shop.

"No way! Last one to the beach gets hit for a six!" Sandeep shouted, increasing his speed.

Laughing, we pushed ahead, our cycles moving in sync like a well-coordinated team. The road leading to Arossim was slightly uphill, and our legs burned as we pedaled harder. But the thought of reaching the beach, of feeling the cool breeze and hearing the waves crash, made every effort worth it.

Finally, the first sight of the ocean appeared in the distance, a deep blue stretching endlessly under the sun. The golden sand shimmered, and the coconut trees lining the shore swayed gently. A rush of excitement filled our hearts as we neared our makeshift playground.

The moment our feet touched the sand, we threw our cycles aside and grabbed the bat and ball. The game began instantly. The first ball was bowled, and the match was on.

Cheers erupted, arguments broke out over close calls, and the sound of the bat hitting the ball echoed across the beach. Nothing else mattered in those hours, not school, not exams, not worries about the future. Only cricket, competition, and laughter.

As the sun started setting, the sky turned a brilliant shade of orange and pink. We collapsed onto the sand, exhausted but content. The sweat on our faces felt like a medal of victory. We lay there, staring at the sky, our chests rising and falling with heavy breaths.

Sandeep wiped his forehead. "So, what's everyone doing this summer?"

Excited voices filled the air as one by one, my friends shared their plans.

"I'm going to Mumbai!" Sandeep announced proudly. "Staying at my mama's place. Beach, movie theaters, and the big city life!"

"Nagpur for me," Pawan added. "My dad planned a whole trip. We're visiting tiger reserves and forts!"

Vikram grinned. "Matheran! No cars, only cool air and mountains!"

As each friend spoke, their voices were full of excitement. I listened, my smile slowly fading. I had no plans. No grand trips. No travel stories waiting to happen. Summer had always been about playing cricket, cycling through the streets of Verna, and watching movies late into the night. But suddenly, my usual plans felt... ordinary.

"What about you, Sunil?" Sandeep nudged me.

I forced a smile. "Uh... nothing decided yet."

Pawan chuckled. "Looks like someone's spending his summer sleeping!"

The group laughed, but I felt something shift inside me. Was this it? Was my summer going to be just another repeat of last year? No new places, no new experiences? The thought left a strange emptiness in my chest.

As we packed up our things and walked back home, I lagged behind the others, lost in thought. The cool evening breeze brushed against my face, and the distant sound of church bells rang in the air. The streets of Verna, which had felt so welcoming in the afternoon, now felt a little smaller, a little quieter.

I didn't want this summer to be just another summer. I wanted something new, something exciting. I wanted an adventure.

But what adventure could a boy from Verna have?

As I cycled back home that evening, the excitement of the day slowly faded into a dull uneasiness. The thought of summer stretched before me like an empty road, and for the first time, I felt left behind. My friends had exciting places to go, new adventures waiting for them, and I had nothing. The ride home was quiet, my thoughts louder than the wind rustling through the coconut trees lining the roads of Verna.

By the time I reached home, the familiar scent of fresh fish curry greeted me at the door. It was almost 8:00 PM, the usual dinner time, and my mom was busy in the kitchen, her hands expertly moving between the steaming pots. The comforting aroma of spices filled the air, making my stomach rumble. My father, as usual, was seated at the dining table, completely engrossed in his legal papers, flipping through thick files, underlining points, and scribbling notes. He barely noticed as I walked in, his mind deep in his work.

I washed my hands and sat down, absently picking at my food. My mother served a generous portion of rice and fish curry onto my plate, her eyes briefly glancing at me.

She noticed my lack of enthusiasm but said nothing. My father was still lost in his documents, occasionally adjusting his glasses as he made notes in the margins.

My sister, on the other hand, was quick to notice. She leaned forward with a smirk. "You look like you just lost a cricket match," she teased.

I sighed, pushing a piece of fish around my plate. "Not funny."

She raised an eyebrow. "So, how was your exam?"

I stiffened slightly, glancing at my father, who was within earshot. The last thing I wanted was a detailed discussion about my exam in front of him.

"It was fine," I said quickly, keeping my voice neutral.

She wasn't convinced. "Fine? That's all you're going to say? Which subject was it today? What questions came? Did you finish everything?" She fired off questions faster than I could think.

I shot her a warning glance. "Stop asking so many questions! It was good, alright? Just let it go."

She chuckled, leaning back in her chair. "Okay, okay. Touchy much?"

My father finally locked up from his papers, glancing at me over the rim of his glasses. "If the exam went well, then that's all that matters," he said simply before returning to his work.

I exhaled, relieved that the topic was over. But my sister wasn't done with me yet.

She watched me carefully as I played with my food, her smirk fading into curiosity. "You seem distracted. What's going on?"

I hesitated for a moment, then sighed. "Sandeep and Pawan are going on trips this summer. Sandeep is off to Mumbai, and Pawan is heading to Nagpur with his family.

Vikram is going to Matheran. Everyone has plans... except me."

Mom glanced at me as she sat down, a knowing look on her face. "And that bothers you?"

I shrugged. "I don't know. It just feels like I'm going to be stuck here doing nothing while they're out having fun."

My sister leaned forward, a mischievous smile dancing on her lips. "I have an idea," she said, tapping her fingers against the table.

I gave her a skeptical look. "What now?"

She grinned. "Why don't you do something different this summer instead of just staying home and playing cricket?"

I rolled my eyes. "Like what? There's nothing exciting to do here."

Mom wiped her hands on her apron and sat down beside me. "Your sister is right, Sunil. There's always something new to learn. Maybe you just haven't thought about it yet."

Dad put his pen down and finally looked at me, his sharp eyes observing me with a knowing expression. "You don't have to sit idle. You could always do something new."

I let out a frustrated sigh. "Like what?" I repeated, staring at my half-eaten food.

My sister smirked. "What if I told you there's a summer camp happening in Panjim?"

I blinked. "Summer camp?"

She nodded excitedly. "Yes! It's in St. Thomas High School. They have everything, computers, yoga, karate, drama, dance... And guess what? Prathamesh is going too."

My ears perked up at the mention of Prathamesh. He had been my friend since childhood. If he was going, maybe it wouldn't be so bad.

Mom noticed my hesitation. "It's for fifteen days, Sunil. It will be a great experience for you."

Dad leaned back in his chair. "Discipline, independence, and learning something new, sounds like a good way to spend your summer."

I thought about it for a moment. The idea of being away from home, of doing something different, of experiencing something new, it all felt overwhelming yet thrilling at the same time.

"Panjim, huh?" I murmured, picturing the bustling city, the wide roads, the busy markets, and the idea of being in a place filled with people I didn't know.

My sister grinned. "Yes! And trust me, you won't regret it."

For the first time since the conversation started, I felt a small spark of excitement. Maybe this summer wasn't going to be as boring as I thought.

That night, as I lay in bed staring at the ceiling, my mind was no longer filled with the disappointment of being left behind. Instead, I imagined days filled with adventure, meeting new people, and learning things I had never tried before.

Maybe this summer was going to be different. Maybe it was going to change my life in ways I hadn't even imagined.

The next morning, I woke up feeling refreshed. A sense of anticipation filled me as I went downstairs. Mom was already awake, preparing breakfast, while Dad was on the telephone discussing a case with one of his clients. His deep voice carried through the room as he spoke about legal matters, scribbling notes onto a sheet of paper beside him. My sister sat at the table, flipping through an old magazine, occasionally tapping her fingers on the wooden surface.

She looked up as I sat down. "So, are you going to summer camp or not?" she asked, reaching for a slice of toast.

I nodded. "I think I am."

A satisfied smile spread across her face. "Good. I'll talk to Prathamesh's parents and make sure you both get enrolled together."

TWO

<u>Journey to Panjim</u>

The long-awaited day had finally arrived. After three days of anticipation, Monday morning had come, bringing with it an excitement that made my heart race. I had barely slept the night before, my mind filled with thoughts of what lay ahead. A new place, new people, and two whole weeks of adventure, this summer was going to be different.

The morning sun peeked through my window, casting a golden glow across my room. The air was warm yet carried a light coastal breeze, the scent of the sea mingling with the fragrance of wet earth from the previous night's drizzle. Goa's monsoon season was approaching, and the sky was a mix of soft blue and scattered clouds, promising a day of unpredictable weather.

I jumped out of bed, barely able to contain my excitement. My mother was already in the kitchen, preparing breakfast, her bangles clinking softly as she moved between the pots and pans. The familiar aroma of freshly brewed tea and hot poha filled the air. As I entered the kitchen, she turned with a smile, wiping her hands on her saree.

"Today is the big day, Sunil! Are you excited?" she asked, setting a plate of steaming poha in front of me.

I grinned, stuffing a spoonful into my mouth. "Very excited! I just want to reach Panjim already."

She chuckled and ruffled my hair. "Not so fast. You still need to pack the last few things. I've made some food for you to take along, some bebinca, chorizo pav, and cashew nuts. You'll miss home food when you're away."

I smiled. My mother always knew how to take care of me. She had woken up early to prepare my favorite dishes, just so I wouldn't feel homesick.

After breakfast, we moved to my room where my suitcase lay open on the bed. She helped me fold my clothes neatly, making sure I had everything I needed. Shirts, shorts, socks, and my favorite blue towel were all tucked in carefully. She placed the food at the top, reminding me to share it with Prathamesh.

Outside, the sounds of the town waking up filled the air. The distant ringing of church bells, the honking of scooters passing by, and the faint chatter of fisherwomen setting up their stalls near the market, all familiar sounds that I had grown up with. But today, they felt different. Today, they felt like a farewell.

My father entered my room, adjusting his wristwatch. "All set, Sunil?" he asked, his deep voice steady as always.

I nodded. "Yes, Dad. Everything is packed."

He placed a hand on my shoulder and gave me a firm nod. "Good. Make the most of this trip. Learn something new and have fun. And remember to behave well."

I smiled. "I will."

With my bag finally packed and my heart full of anticipation, I was ready. Outside, our Maruti 800 stood washed and gleaming, its white paint shining in the morning sun. My father had taken extra care to clean it for the journey, making sure everything was set for a smooth ride. The air smelled fresh, the day had begun, and I couldn't wait to start my adventure.

As our Maruti 800 cruised down the highway, the wind blew against my face through the half-open window. The scent of the sea mixed with the warm summer air. Goa had always been beautiful, but today, it felt different, like the beginning of something I didn't fully understand yet.

"Excited?" my father asked, glancing at me through the rear-view mirror.

I nodded. "Yeah... but a little nervous too."

He smiled. "That's good. A little nervousness means something important is about to happen."

I looked outside, watching the coconut trees sway gently against the bright blue sky. The road ahead stretched endlessly, winding through lush green fields and small villages where early risers were beginning their day. Women stood outside their homes, drying clothes on lines, while men gathered in small tea stalls, sipping chai and chatting about the latest news.

As we passed by, I saw fishermen along the riverbanks, their boats anchored, as they prepared for another day at sea. The sound of birds chirping and distant church bells echoed in the air, adding a serene rhythm to our journey.

Our car moved smoothly along the highway, passing through tunnels carved into the rocky hillsides. The sunlight flickered through the car window, creating a dance of light and shadow on my face. Every few kilometers, we would see roadside vendors selling fresh coconuts, their carts lined with stacks of green husks.

"Do you want one?" Dad asked, slowing the car near a vendor.

I nodded eagerly. He pulled over, and within moments, a man expertly chopped the top off a coconut, handing it to me with a straw. The sweet, cool water refreshed me instantly.

As we continued, the scenery became even more mesmerizing. Hills covered in thick forests stood proudly against the sky, their tops kissed by drifting clouds. The air smelled of fresh rain, and I took a deep breath, savoring the scent of nature mixed with the salty ocean breeze.

"We'll stop at the Miramar viewpoint," Dad said. "You'll love the view of the Mandovi River."

I nodded excitedly. The thought of seeing Panjim from a high point filled me with anticipation. As we approached, the river came into sight, its calm waters reflecting the golden rays of the sun. Boats moved lazily across the surface, and the city skyline of Panjim stood tall in the distance.

We parked near the viewpoint and stepped out. The breeze was stronger here, carrying the sound of the waves crashing against the shore. I leaned against the railing, staring out at the horizon, feeling the enormity of the world in front of me.

"This is just the beginning, Sunil," Dad said, placing a hand on my shoulder.

I smiled, feeling a sense of adventure rise within me. The journey to Panjim was more than just a trip; it was the start of something new, something that would stay with me forever.

As we got back into the car, I felt a renewed excitement bubbling inside me. The road ahead was full of possibilities, and I was ready to embrace them all.

The car moved smoothly along the bridge that connected us to the heart of Panjim. The Mandovi River stretched wide beneath us, the water glistening under the sunlight. Ferry boats moved along the river, carrying people from one side to the other, their slow pace adding a rhythm to the city's life.

As we entered the city, the quiet roads of Verna faded behind us. The streets of Panjim were alive, buses honked, motorbikes zipped past, and people hurried across the roads. The architecture was a beautiful mix of Portuguese and Indian influences, with old, colorful houses standing side by side with modern buildings.

Dad pointed towards a grand white church standing atop a hill. "That's the Our Lady of the Immaculate Conception Church. One of Panjim's most famous spots. We'll visit it sometime."

I nodded, already in awe of the vibrant energy around me. The city felt so different from the slow-paced life of Verna. Here, everything moved faster, yet there was something charming about it. The small bakeries selling warm pão (bread), the street vendors calling out their prices, the sight of tourists walking around, cameras in hand, it was all new and exciting.

We made our way through the narrow lanes, passing by old cafés and bookstores. The smell of freshly brewed coffee mixed with the aroma of spices from roadside stalls. The bright afternoon sun cast long shadows on the streets, and the warmth of the day made the colors of the city appear even richer.

Dad pulled the car over near a tea stall, and we stepped out for a short break. The air was thick with the scent of freshly brewed chai and fried snacks sizzling in large pans. A man served hot tea in small glasses, and Dad handed me one. The warm tea was a perfect companion to the bustling energy around us.

"Feels nice, doesn't it?" Dad said, sipping his tea.

I nodded, watching the busy street, the sound of conversations mixing with the distant honking of vehicles. "Yeah... it really does."

After a brief pause, we got back into the car and continued driving, the heart of Panjim welcoming us with its endless charm.

Soon, we reached the gates of St. Thomas High School, my home for the next fifteen days. My heart pounded with nervous excitement. I felt my stomach tighten. The school was massive, with tall white buildings standing proudly under the afternoon sun. The playground stretched wide, covered in fresh green grass where groups of students gathered, chatting and laughing. The air buzzed with excitement, a mixture of nervous energy and anticipation for the days ahead.

Dad parked the car near the entrance, and I could see students dragging their suitcases, some looking as nervous as I felt. A large banner near the gate read: **Welcome to St. Thomas High School Summer Camp!** My heart pounded in my chest.

Dad turned to me with a reassuring smile. "Sunil, welcome to your home for the next two weeks." He patted my back, giving me an encouraging nod.

I took a deep breath, swallowing my nervousness, and stepped out of the car. The ground felt firm under my feet, but my legs felt wobbly. This was it. A new place, new faces, and an adventure I had no idea would change me forever.

We made our way to the registration desk, where a teacher wearing thick glasses sat behind a wooden table. She looked up and smiled warmly. "Name?"

"Sunil," I said quickly, my voice slightly shaky.

She checked her list and nodded. "Room B-12. You'll be staying with two other boys. Here's your key. Welcome,

Sunil."

I took the key from her, glancing back at Dad. He looked at me for a moment, as if studying my face, then placed a firm hand on my shoulder. "Have fun, Sunil. Enjoy every moment."

And just like that, he was gone.

I stood there, feeling alone for the first time. A lump formed in my throat. All around me, kids were laughing, finding their friends, running toward their dorms. I was about to let the nervousness take over when a familiar voice called from behind me.

"Hey, Sunil!"

I turned around, and my face instantly lit up. "Prathamesh!"

He grinned, pulling me into a quick hug. "I'm so glad you came, man! I was worried you'd back out."

His energy was infectious. Instantly, my nervousness vanished. I had a friend here. This was going to be good.

We grabbed our bags and headed towards the dormitory. The corridor echoed with voices and footsteps, kids dragging their suitcases, parents giving last-minute instructions. It smelled of fresh paint and wooden furniture, and a cool breeze from the open windows made the place feel welcoming.

Room B-12 was on the first floor. As we stepped inside, I noticed three beds, neatly arranged against the walls, a large window overlooking the playground, and a cupboard for each of us. The afternoon sunlight poured in through the window, making the room feel bright and airy.

Just as I placed my bag on the bed, the door opened, and our third roommate walked in. He was tall, with glasses and a confident smile. He carried himself with an ease that suggested he wasn't new to places like this.

"Hey, I'm Rohit," he said, shaking my hand firmly.

"Sunil," I introduced myself.

Prathamesh clapped his hands together. "Alright, boys! We have two weeks of freedom. Let's make it legendary!"

I laughed, feeling the excitement grow inside me. This was going to be fun.

That evening, we attended an orientation session in the school's grand auditorium. The hall was filled with excited campers. A senior teacher welcomed us, explaining the schedule, activities, and rules. There would be sports, drama, music, and even a talent show at the end of the camp. The energy in the room was electrifying.

After the session, we made our way back to the dormitory. The hallway was alive with chatter and laughter. Some kids were already making plans for the next day, while others unpacked and settled into their rooms.

As we reached our room, Rohit stretched his arms. "First day almost done. What do you guys want to do now?"

Prathamesh grinned. "Let's go explore the campus! It's huge!"

I hesitated for a second, but then I nodded. "Let's do it."

We stepped out into the cool night air. The sky was dark, but the campus lights illuminated the pathways. The school looked even bigger now, with its towering buildings and vast playgrounds. We walked past the library, the cafeteria, and the sports complex, taking in everything.

"This place is amazing," I said, feeling a rush of excitement.

"Yeah, and for two weeks, it's ours," Rohit added with a grin.

We continued walking, breathing in the night air, feeling the thrill of something new. The nervousness I had felt earlier was gone. Now, there was only excitement, adventure, and the promise of an unforgettable summer.

As we returned to our room, I looked around at my new friends and my new home for the next two weeks. A smile crept onto my face.

Yes. This was going to be an experience I would never forget.

THREE

A Moment That Felt Like Forever

The next morning, the first day of camp officially began. At exactly 7:00 AM, a loud bell rang through the corridors, jolting me awake. For a moment, I forgot where I was. Then, as my eyes adjusted to the dim morning light, I remembered, I was at St. Thomas High School, and the summer camp had officially started.

I stretched and looked around. Prathamesh was still half-asleep, groaning as he pulled his blanket over his head. Rohit, on the other hand, was already up, neatly folding his blanket.

"Come on, guys! We have to get to the assembly area," Rohit reminded us, tying his shoelaces.

I rubbed my eyes and sat up. "Yeah, yeah... I'm up."

The night before, during orientation, we were told that everyone had to gather in the assembly area first thing in the morning. No excuses. No delays. It was the official start of our summer camp experience.

I quickly freshened up and dressed in a simple t-shirt and track pants. Within minutes, we joined the stream of students heading towards the assembly area. The cool morning air was refreshing, carrying the faint scent of wet grass and fresh earth. The sun had just begun to rise, casting a golden glow over the campus.

As we reached the large open ground, I saw that nearly 150 to 200 students had already gathered. Everyone was between the ages of 15 and 18. I was 17 at the time, and so was Prathamesh. The air buzzed with excitement, murmurs of conversation, and sleepy yawns. I stood next to Prathamesh, scanning the crowd. It was a sea of faces, some familiar from the night before, others completely new.

Then, the instructor walked onto the small stage in front of us. She was a tall, confident woman with a sharp voice that commanded attention. She held a mic in her hand and smiled as she looked over the large group.

"Good morning, everyone!" she said, her voice loud and clear.

"Good morning, ma'am!" we all responded in unison.

She nodded approvingly. "Welcome to St. Thomas High School Summer Camp! Over the next 15 days, you are going to experience something truly special. This is not just a camp, it's a journey of learning, fun, and self-discovery."

I listened carefully, eager to know what was planned for us.

"This camp is designed to help you develop new skills, explore your talents, and build friendships that will last a lifetime," she continued. "Now, let me introduce you to some of the activities you'll be participating in."

She gestured to her left, where a group of teachers and instructors stood.

"First, we have computer classes. Computers are the future, and we want you to get familiar with this new technology. Each of you will get a chance to work in our computer lab. Whether you're a beginner or have some experience, we will ensure that you learn something new."

My ears perked up. Computers had always fascinated me, but I had never gotten the chance to actually work on one. In 2004, having access to a computer was a big deal. I couldn't wait to get my hands on a keyboard.

"Next, we have dance classes!" the instructor announced. "Meet our dance instructors."

A group of young men and women stepped forward, waving at us. Some students cheered, already excited.

"Whether you're a trained dancer or have two left feet, this class is for everyone. You'll learn different styles, have fun, and maybe even perform at the end of the camp!" she said with a grin.

I exchanged a glance with Prathamesh, who raised an eyebrow. "Dancing? Not really my thing."

I chuckled. "Same here. But let's see."

The instructor continued, "We also have yoga and karate sessions. Physical fitness is important, and these activities will help improve your focus, discipline, and strength."

At the mention of karate, a ripple of excitement ran through the crowd. Many students whispered among themselves, eager to try something new.

I stood there, listening carefully, taking in every word. The schedule sounded exciting, filled with so many things I had never done before.

But then, in the middle of it all, my eyes got stuck on one girl.

I hadn't noticed her before, but now, it was as if everything around me faded. She stood near the front, her long hair falling neatly over her shoulders. She was listening to the instructor with a soft smile, her eyes focused, her presence calm yet striking.

For a moment, I forgot about the camp, the classes, and the crowd. The only thing I could think about was, who was she?

And just like that, my summer camp had suddenly become a lot more interesting.

After the morning session ended, time seemed to move faster than I expected. The sun was now high in the sky, casting golden light over the campus. It was around 2:00 PM when the bell rang for the lunch break. The energy of the camp had settled into a more relaxed hum, with students making their way toward the dining hall.

Prathamesh and I decided to step outside for some fresh air before heading for lunch. The day had been exciting, but something inside me felt restless, like I was waiting for something... or someone.

And then, it happened.

As we walked toward the canteen, my eyes landed on her.

She was standing beneath an old oak tree, a soft breeze playing with the loose strands of her long, dark hair. She was talking to a group of girls, her laughter ringing through the air like the sweetest melody. It wasn't forced or loud, it was natural, effortless, the kind of laugh that made the world stop for just a second.

I felt something shift inside me, like the air had changed, like the universe had pressed pause just for me to look at her.

"Who's that?" I asked, my voice barely above a whisper, as if speaking too loudly would break the spell she had unknowingly cast on me.

Prathamesh followed my gaze and smirked knowingly. "That's Nutan. She's from Mapusa. First time at this camp, like you."

Nutan.

I repeated the name in my head, and it felt like poetry, like something I wanted to say again and again. A name that wasn't just a name anymore, it was a feeling, a sensation, a heartbeat.

I couldn't look away. Everything else blurred, the students walking by, the voices around me, even the sun overhead. All I could see was her.

And then... she turned.

For a second, just a fleeting, delicate second, our eyes met.

It wasn't just a glance. It was a moment, one that wrapped around me like a warm breeze. Her eyes held something I couldn't explain, kindness, curiosity, a world I suddenly wanted to be a part of.

And then... she smiled.

Not just any smile. It was the kind of smile that made the first raindrop feel magical after months of heat. The kind that felt like music, like the first notes of a song that you know will stay with you forever.

I had no idea what was happening inside me. My heart raced, my breath caught, and for the first time in my life, words failed me. I had never believed in stories where people felt something in an instant, but standing there, frozen in time, I knew, this moment would never leave me.

I didn't know what it meant. I didn't know what would happen next.

All I knew was this, this summer had just become something I would never forget.

I watched as she tucked a loose strand of hair behind her ear, her delicate fingers moving as if time itself had slowed down. The wind lifted the ends of her dress slightly, making it dance around her knees, and for a brief second, she looked like something out of a forgotten love story, timeless, untouched, unreal.

And then... she turned.

Her gaze met mine, and the world stopped.

A single moment, stretched across eternity.

Her deep brown eyes locked onto mine, and suddenly, the air around me felt heavier, charged with something unexplainable. It was like being caught in a silent storm, where nothing moved except the unspoken words between us.

Did she feel it too?

Or was it just me?

Her lips curled into a soft smile, the kind that felt like the first raindrop after months of summer heat. It wasn't exaggerated or forced, it was simple, warm, real.

And just like that, I was lost.

A rush of something unnameable filled my chest, something I had never felt before. My breath hitched, my fingers curled, and my heart, my heart no longer belonged to me.

She had stolen it.

In one glance. In one smile. Without even trying.

I stood there, frozen, wondering if this was what people meant when they talked about destiny.

But then... the moment shattered.

A shadow stepped between us, breaking the invisible thread that had connected us for those few fleeting seconds.

Sheetal.

She moved like a storm, her sharp eyes brimming with something unspoken, something that warned me before she even spoke.

She turned towards Nutan, placing a hand on her arm, possessive, protective. And then she looked at me.

That look was enough to tell me what she wanted to say.

Stay away.

I swallowed hard, the weight of reality crashing into me like a wave. I wasn't welcome in their world. Not yet. Maybe not ever.

Behind her, Nutan's smile faltered, just for a second, like she wanted to say something. Like she didn't want the moment to end.

But Sheetal had already decided.

She took Nutan's hand, turned her away from me, and in just a few steps... she was gone.

I let out a breath I hadn't realized I was holding, my chest suddenly feeling empty, like something had been taken from me before I even had the chance to claim it.

The warmth of the moment disappeared. The air felt colder now, heavier, as if I had just woken up from the sweetest dream, only to realize I could never go back to it.

Prathamesh sighed beside me, shaking his head. "Well," he muttered, "that was... intense."

I didn't respond. I couldn't.

Because even as I stood there, watching the girl beneath the oak tree walk away, my heart knew one thing for sure.

This wasn't over.

Not yet.

FOUR

The Wall

The night had fallen over the summer camp, but my mind was still stuck in that one moment beneath the oak tree. The camp was alive with the soft rustling of leaves, distant laughter from groups of students still awake, and the occasional ringing of the camp bell. But none of it mattered to me.

I lay on my bed in the dimly lit dorm room, my hands tucked under my head, staring at the ceiling as if it could answer the millions of questions racing through my mind. The faint glow from the bedside lamp cast long shadows across the room, but the only image my mind kept replaying was her.

Nutan.

That one smile, the way her lips curved ever so softly, like she knew something I didn't. It wasn't just any smile; it was a moment, a feeling, a spark that burned its way into my memory, refusing to leave. I tried to close my eyes, but every time I did, I saw her again, standing beneath that tree, her long hair catching the last golden rays of the sun.

I turned to the side, restless, my heart still hammering from the way she had looked at me. Did she feel it too? Or was I just another face in the crowd, another fleeting moment in her world? A sigh escaped my lips as I ran a hand through my hair, frustration creeping in.

But just as my heart soared at the thought of Nutan, another face flashed before my eyes.

Sheetal.

Her cold, piercing gaze.

Unlike Nutan's warmth, Sheetal's eyes held something else, something unreadable. A silent wall, standing firm between me and the girl who had unknowingly captured my thoughts. The way she had stepped forward, shielding Nutan from me before I could even take a step closer.

I let out a long breath. This wasn't going to be easy.

The camp bell rang early in the morning, announcing the start of a new day. The sun had barely kissed the horizon when I pulled myself out of bed, stretching away the thoughts that had kept me awake.

Today was the day. I would talk to her. I would find a way to be closer to Nutan.

As I made my way to the common area, students filled the pathways, their voices blending into a morning hum of excitement and new beginnings. The air smelled of freshly watered grass and the faint aroma of breakfast from the mess hall.

And then, my eyes found her.

Nutan.

She sat on a stone bench near the garden, the sunlight dancing across her features as she tossed her head back in laughter. A few strands of her dark hair fell over her shoulder, and she tucked them behind her ear absentmindedly. The world around her seemed to slow down as I watched, captivated.

My feet moved before my mind could catch up. I didn't think, I didn't plan, I just knew I had to talk to her.

But just as I took another step,

Sheetal appeared.

Like a shadow that refused to fade, she was there before I could even reach Nutan. Her presence was deliberate, calculated, as if she had been expecting me. Her eyes met mine, unwavering, assessing.

I stopped in my tracks, the silent message in her stare freezing me in place.

This wasn't just a casual encounter.

This was a warning.

She tilted her head slightly, arms crossed over her chest, her expression unreadable. "You're looking for someone?" Her voice was calm, but there was an edge to it, a quiet strength, an unspoken challenge.

I cleared my throat, willing myself to appear unaffected. "Uh... yeah. I was just, "

"Nutan is busy."

The words were simple, direct. But the weight behind them told me everything I needed to know.

I glanced past her, towards Nutan, who was still chatting with her friends, completely unaware of the silent battle unfolding just a few feet away.

I looked back at Sheetal.

She wasn't angry. She wasn't aggressive.

But she was firm.

She had already decided something about me. And whatever it was, it wasn't in my favor.

I forced a small smile, as if this exchange meant nothing. "I just wanted to say hi."

Sheetal didn't move. She didn't blink. She just stood there, a silent guardian, blocking my path without lifting a finger.

And in that moment, I realized,

I had an enemy.

Not because of something I had done. But because Sheetal had already made up her mind about me. And if I wanted to be close to Nutan...

I would have to go through Sheetal first.

The next few days at camp felt like a game I wasn't sure I knew how to play. Every time I saw Nutan, Sheetal was there. If Nutan was walking toward the dance hall, Sheetal was walking beside her. If Nutan was sitting in the canteen, Sheetal was right across from her. If Nutan laughed at something, Sheetal was always the first one to react, making sure no one else got too close.

And me?

I was left watching from a distance, stuck on the outside of their little world.

It was frustrating. Every time I tried to speak to Nutan, Sheetal found a way to interrupt.

"Hey, Nutan!" I called out one afternoon when I saw her alone.

She turned, her eyes lighting up for a second, Before Sheetal suddenly appeared beside her.

"Nutan, we have to go. Now."

Nutan hesitated, glancing at me.

But then, she nodded and left with Sheetal.

And just like that, another chance was lost.

The days at camp had started to feel like a silent battle, one where every step I took towards Nutan was met with an invisible barrier named Sheetal. She had made it clear that I wasn't welcome, that whatever existed between me and Nutan would never have the chance to bloom. And for days, I felt like I was running in circles, watching from the outside, unable to step into Nutan's world.

But then, something happened.

One evening, after our activities had ended, I found myself walking towards the garden, lost in thought. The sky had started to melt into warm hues of orange and pink, casting long shadows over the camp. The air was still, carrying the scent of fresh grass and damp earth.

And then I saw her.

Nutan.

She was sitting alone on the wooden bench, her notebook resting on her lap. A few loose strands of her hair moved gently in the breeze as she absentmindedly flipped through the pages, completely unaware of the world around her.

There was no Sheetal in sight.

My heart pounded. This was my chance.

I took a deep breath, steadied my nerves, and walked towards her. My footsteps felt heavier with every step, my mind filled with uncertainty. Would she acknowledge me? Would she turn away? Would Sheetal suddenly appear and pull her away before I could even say a word?

I hesitated for a second before speaking. "Hey, Nutan."

She looked up.

For a brief moment, there was surprise in her eyes. But then... she smiled.

It wasn't just any smile. It was warm, soft, and inviting. The kind of smile that made me forget all the struggles of the past few days. The kind that made everything feel worth it.

"Hi, Sunil," she said softly.

My name. She had said my name.

And in that small moment, under the fading glow of the evening sun, something shifted inside me.

Maybe Sheetal was a wall.

Maybe she was going to make this difficult.

But this moment... this connection...
This was worth fighting for.

FIVE

The Rain

The sky had been restless since the afternoon. The scorching summer heat that had clung to Goa for months had started to ease, replaced by a strange, electric stillness. By 4:00 PM, the wind had begun to change, carrying with it a scent so distinct, so intoxicating, the scent of rain before it arrives. The trees swayed, the birds flew lower, and the golden hues of the evening sky slowly turned into deep shades of gray.

It was a promise. A promise that the first rain of the season was coming.

At the summer camp, excitement hummed in the air. Kids whispered about the changing weather, some hoping for rain, others skeptical. But I knew. I could feel it in my bones. The earth was waiting. The sky was waiting. And, maybe, just maybe, so was my heart.

The entire day had passed in a blur, morning karate sessions, afternoon computer lessons, evening sports. But my mind had been elsewhere. With her.

Nutan.

Her name had settled in my heart like a melody that refused to fade. It wasn't just that I had spoken to her for the first time. It was the way she had said my name. Softly. As if she had known me forever.

That moment had played in my mind over and over again, the way she had looked up from her notebook, the way she had smiled when she saw me. It wasn't just a smile; it was something more. A silent invitation into a world I desperately wanted to be a part of.

But there was always Sheetal.

Always watching. Always making sure I didn't get too close. A shadow between me and Nutan, guarding her like a protective sister, or maybe something else.

But tonight... tonight, the universe had other plans.

It started as a whisper.

A distant rumble echoed across the sky, rolling over the hills, making its way toward us. The wind picked up speed, rustling through the camp, lifting dry leaves into the air. The lanterns around the courtyard flickered, their golden glow trembling against the sudden chill that crept in.

And then...

The first raindrop.

It landed on my arm, cool and fresh against my warm skin. A second later, another. Then another. And before I could even register the moment, the heavens broke open.

The summer rain arrived like a long-lost lover, drenching the parched earth, filling the air with the scent of wet soil, the scent of new beginnings.

The camp erupted in chaos.

Some campers screamed and ran for shelter. Others cheered, stretching their arms out, welcoming the downpour. Laughter, excitement, freedom, all wrapped in the sound of raindrops hitting the ground.

And then...

Through the blurred curtain of rain, I saw her. Nutan stood in the courtyard, untouched by the commotion around her. She tilted her head back, eyes closed, her hands outstretched, letting the rain kiss her skin.

She wasn't running for cover.

She was dancing.

Slowly. Freely. Her dark hair clung to her face, her dress soaked, tracing every curve of her body. She twirled under the sky as if the rain had been meant just for her. As if the universe had conspired to bring this exact moment to life.

And I stood there, mesmerized.

The world around me blurred. The voices faded. The hundred campers, the rules, Sheetal's watchful eyes, none of it mattered anymore.

All that mattered was her.

And suddenly, I couldn't hold back any longer.

Something inside me broke free, a hesitation, a fear, an unspoken rule.

I took a step forward.

Then another.

And before I knew it, I was walking toward her, the rain drenching me, my heart pounding against my ribs.

Tonight, I wasn't going to let this moment slip away.

Before I could even think twice, my feet started moving, drawn to her as if the rain itself had whispered my name, urging me forward. The world blurred around me, the voices of campers fading into the rhythmic sound of raindrops hitting the earth.

She turned just as I reached her, her deep brown eyes locking onto mine. And then... she smiled.

That same smile. The one that made me forget who I was, where I was. A smile that felt like a secret meant only for me.

"Sunil," she said, her voice barely audible over the rain, yet it reached straight to my soul.

I swallowed, trying to steady my breath. "Do you always dance in the rain?"

She let out a soft laugh, tilting her head slightly. "Only when it feels special."

Something inside me flipped.

Special.

This moment was special.

She turned away slightly, closing her eyes as the rain kissed her skin, a peaceful expression settling on her face. It was as if she was absorbing the storm, letting it become a part of her. And in that moment, I wanted to be a part of it too.

I didn't think. I just felt.

I stepped closer, my heart hammering in my chest, my hand reaching out before I could stop myself.

"Dance with me?"

She opened her eyes, surprise flickering across her face. For a moment, she didn't move.

And then...

She placed her hand in mine.

A rush of warmth spread through me despite the cold rain. Her fingers were soft, delicate, fitting perfectly against mine, as if they had always belonged there. I pulled her gently, and just like that, we danced. Not like those perfect lovers in the movies, not like trained dancers who knew every step. No, we stumbled, we laughed, we moved as if the world had melted away, leaving only us.

She twirled once, and I caught her hand before she could slip. I stepped too fast, and she giggled, trying to match my pace. The rain wrapped around us, the sound of thunder echoing in the distance, but I wasn't afraid.

Because in this moment, with her in my arms, with her laughter filling the air, I felt something I had never felt before.

I felt alive.

I felt complete.

I had dreamed of moments like this. Moments that didn't need words, didn't need promises, just feelings. And in this rain, in this dance, I knew.

This wasn't just a summer crush.

This was something deeper. Something that would linger in my heart long after the rain had stopped.

But just as I started to believe this moment was truly ours, just as I started to believe she was mine,

She arrived.

Like a sudden gust of cold wind, like the final bell that ends a beautiful dream.

Sheetal.

Her eyes were sharp, her expression unreadable, but her presence alone was enough to shatter the magic in the air. She stood at the edge of the courtyard, her arms crossed, her posture rigid. The rain poured around her, but she remained unaffected, unmoving.

"Nutan."

Her voice was firm. Not angry, not loud, but unshakable.

Nutan froze, her laughter fading, her hand still resting in mine. I felt her hesitate. I felt her wanting to stay. But Sheetal took a step closer, her body language screaming what I already knew.

This moment was over.

"Nutan, let's go."

A pause.

Nutan turned to me, her eyes searching mine. I held my breath. I wanted her to say something. To tell Sheetal she wanted to stay. To tell me this moment meant something to her too.

But she didn't.

She pulled her hand away slowly, gently, like she didn't want to. And with one last glance, she walked away.

Sheetal followed close behind, throwing me one final look. A look that sealed my fate.

A look that said, you'll never have her.

I stood there, the rain still pouring down, the moment crumbling into nothingness.

My hands were empty. But my heart?

It was completely, hopelessly full.

Because for those few minutes, Nutan was mine.

And for the rest of my life... I would never forget the night we danced in the rain.

The night after the rain felt different. The world was still the same, the camp still buzzed with excited voices, the schedule of activities remained unchanged, and the warm Goan breeze still carried the scent of the ocean. But something inside me had shifted.

I had danced with Nutan.

For those few minutes, she had been mine.

The way she had held my hand, the way she had laughed in the rain, the way her eyes had searched for something in mine before she walked away, it had left an ache inside me that I couldn't explain.

I couldn't stop thinking about it. I couldn't stop thinking about her.

And every time I closed my eyes, I could still feel the rain, still hear her laughter, still wish that moment had never ended.

But Sheetal...

Sheetal had made sure it did.

She had pulled Nutan away, breaking the spell, taking her back to a world where I didn't exist.

And now, I had no idea where I stood.

Did Nutan feel the same?

Did that moment mean something to her the way it had meant everything to me?

Or was I just a boy falling too fast for something that was never his?

SIX

The Announcement

The next morning, the campgrounds buzzed with the usual energy, footsteps crunching against gravel, the murmurs of half-awake campers, the crisp morning air filled with the scent of damp earth from last night's rain. But today, there was something else in the air. Something electric.

One of the instructors clapped his hands, gathering us in the open-air assembly area. "Alright, campers! Tomorrow night, we're having a singing competition!"

A wave of excitement rippled through the crowd. Murmurs turned into animated whispers, plans forming as people huddled in small groups. Some already knew what they would sing, others debated forming duets. For most, it was a chance to showcase their talent, to laugh, to create memories that would last far beyond this summer.

I wasn't interested.

Until...

"Nutan, you should sing!" someone called out from the crowd.

My heart stopped.

A few rows ahead, Nutan turned, her eyebrows raising in surprise. She let out a light laugh, shaking her head. "Me? I don't know..."

"Come on, Nutan!" another voice chimed in. "You have such a beautiful voice!"

I held my breath.

Would she say yes?

Would I get to hear her voice?

The air felt charged, like the moment before a first drop of rain. Her hesitation was fleeting, her smile hesitant yet undeniable. Then, after what felt like an eternity, she nodded.

"Alright... I'll sing."

The crowd cheered, voices blending into a symphony of encouragement, but I barely heard any of it. Because in that instant, my heartbeat changed its rhythm.

Tomorrow night, I would hear Nutan sing.

And I had a feeling this wasn't just going to be a song.

This was going to be a moment.

The next day passed in a blur. The hours stretched endlessly, yet I couldn't recall a single thing I did. Karate practice? I went through the motions. Computer class? I stared at the screen without really seeing it. Meals? I barely tasted a bite.

Because all I could think about was the fact that tonight, Nutan would sing.

And I wasn't ready for it.

Somehow, deep down, I already knew, this wasn't going to be just about music. It was going to be something more. Something that would change everything.

And I wasn't sure if I was ready to feel that way.

The night had wrapped itself in a dream-like haze, the air filled with an intoxicating blend of nostalgia and anticipation. The open-air auditorium was alive with flickering fairy lights, casting golden hues over the sea of eager faces. A soft evening breeze carried the faint scent of blooming flowers, mixing with the murmurs of excited whispers and laughter. It was an ordinary camp evening for some. But for me, this night held a weight unlike any other.

Because tonight, she would sing.

The performances had begun. One by one, campers stepped onto the small wooden stage, their voices filling the air with old melodies and vibrant Bollywood tunes. Some sang with passion, others stumbled over lyrics, dissolving into giggles, their voices blending with the rustling leaves and the distant sound of waves crashing against the shore.

It was fun. It was meant to be fun.

But for me, it was something else entirely. I was waiting. Waiting for the moment that would steal the very breath from my lungs.

And then, it happened.

"Nutan," the instructor announced, and suddenly, the world around me ceased to exist.

My heart stilled, a shiver ran down my spine, and for the first time in my life, I understood what it meant to feel utterly powerless. Because the second she stepped onto that stage, it was as if time itself paused just to watch her.

She wore a simple white dress, but under the soft glow of the fairy lights, she looked celestial. The gentle sway of the fabric, the way the breeze teased her dark hair, the way she carried herself, it was as though she wasn't walking but floating. I swallowed, my fingers curling into fists, trying to steady the storm brewing within me.

She adjusted the microphone, took a deep breath, and then,

"Main agar saamne... ab bhi aa jaaun..."

The moment her voice filled the air, something inside me shattered.

Her voice wasn't just soft, it was magic, weaving through the night like an old, forgotten lullaby. It held longing, depth, an ache so raw that it settled deep in my bones. She wasn't just singing; she was confessing, telling a story that had never been spoken, one that only the heart could understand.

"Dekhoon bas tumhe..."

I couldn't look away. I couldn't breathe.

Her eyes fluttered closed, lost in the melody, her hands moving with the rhythm, as if the song coursed through her veins, as if she was not just singing, but living it. And then, just for a second, her gaze met mine.

And in that second, I was undone.

I felt a thousand emotions crash over me like an unforgiving tide. The weight of every unsaid word, every unspoken feeling, every silent dream, it was all there, in the way her voice trembled, in the way her lips formed the words, in the way she looked at me as if she, too, was searching for something she couldn't name.

I had spent sleepless nights wondering what it would be like to have her look at me like that, to hold me in her gaze like I was the only one who mattered. And now, here she was, standing on a stage, singing words that felt like they belonged only to us.

This wasn't just a song. This was something else. This was a confession without words, a love letter carried by the wind, a promise that neither of us had the courage to speak aloud.

And just as my heart soared,

The spell broke.

Because when I let my gaze flicker just past Nutan, I saw her.

Sheetal.

She wasn't clapping. She wasn't smiling. She wasn't lost in the music like everyone else. She was staring at me, her dark eyes sharp, her expression cold. And in that silence, in that look, she delivered a message clearer than any words could have.

Stay away.

She is not yours.

You don't belong in her world.

A sharp pain shot through my chest, the warmth that Nutan's voice had built inside me turning to ice.

Because no matter how much I wanted her... no matter how much this moment felt like it belonged to us... the world wouldn't let it be ours.

Nutan kept singing, her voice rising like a gentle whisper against the night, but I was no longer the same.

Because now, there was a storm inside me.

Because now, there was a battle between what my heart wanted and what reality had just reminded me.

When the last note left her lips, the auditorium erupted into applause. People stood, cheering, clapping, shouting praises. The instructors beamed with pride. Nutan smiled, her cheeks flushed, her eyes shining under the glow of the lights.

But I?

I sat frozen, unable to move, unable to join in their cheers.

Because while they had heard a song, I had felt something break inside me.

And I had no idea how to fix it.

SEVEN

The Confession

The summer camp was ending. The thought hit me like a slow, sinking realization, one that I had been trying to push away, but now, with just two days left, there was no running from it. Thirteen days had passed like a dream, beautiful, fleeting, unreal. And soon, it would all be over.

People laughed, joked about how much they would miss this place, made plans to stay in touch. But deep down, we all knew the truth. Life would pull us back to where we belonged. We would return to our schools, our homes, our cities, and this summer, this magical, impossible summer, would become nothing more than a memory, something we would look back on with a smile and say, *"That was a good time."*

But I didn't want this to be just a memory.

Because there was one person I wasn't ready to leave behind. One person who had become more than just a face in the crowd. One person whose presence had turned these days into something unforgettable.

Nutan.

Her name alone felt like a whisper in my heart, a name I had repeated to myself in stolen moments, in quiet breaths, in the spaces between my thoughts. I had spent nights lying awake, thinking about the way she smiled, the way she laughed, the way her eyes held stories I wanted to read over and over again. I had memorized the way she tucked her hair behind her ear when she was lost in thought, the way she danced in the rain that night, free, unguarded, as if she was a part of the storm itself.

For those moments, it had felt like she was mine.

But was she?

Or was I just another face in this summer's crowd? Just another name she would forget once camp was over?

The thought sent a sharp pain through me, a fear that clenched at my chest and made it hard to breathe.

I couldn't let this end without telling her.

It wasn't just a wish anymore, it was a need.

If I left without telling her how I felt, I would regret it for the rest of my life. I couldn't live with the question *What if?* haunting me forever. I couldn't spend years wondering if maybe, just maybe, she had felt the same way too.

But even as the decision settled in my heart, fear held me back.

Not fear of rejection.

Fear of losing what I already had.

Right now, at least she smiled at me. Right now, at least we talked, laughed together, shared moments that felt like something more. But what if I told her and she didn't feel the same? Would everything change? Would she stop looking at me the way she did? Would she pull away? Would I lose her completely?

I didn't know if I was ready for that.

But I also knew that if I let this moment slip away, if I walked away without saying the words that burned inside me, I would lose something even bigger.

I would lose the chance to know. The chance to fight for whatever this was. I had one last shot. One last chance to change fate. I couldn't let it slip away.

The entire day had passed like a hazy dream, each moment slipping through my fingers like sand in an hourglass. I had moved through the routine like a shadow of myself, body present, mind lost elsewhere. The karate drills blurred into a mess of movements I barely registered. The computer lessons were nothing but a series of clicking sounds and flashing screens that I couldn't focus on. Even conversations felt distant, like they were happening in a world separate from mine.

Because my world was centered on just one question, *how do I tell her?*

The weight of it pressed against my chest, making every breath feel heavier. I had imagined it in a thousand different ways. Maybe I would find her during the lunch break, pull her aside, and speak the words softly, away from prying eyes. Or maybe I would wait until the evening, when the sky was painted in colors of goodbye, when the air was cooler, calmer, wrapping around us like a quiet promise. Should I make it spontaneous, let the words tumble out in the middle of a shared laugh? Or should I be serious, let her see the depth of what I felt?

But every time I thought I had found the right moment, it vanished before I could reach for it. Time was slipping away, pulling me toward the inevitable ending I wasn't ready to face. Every time I caught a glimpse of her, laughing with her friends, tucking a strand of hair behind her ear, adjusting the bracelet on her wrist, I felt something tighten in my chest, a desperation, a longing that refused to be silenced.

By the time evening arrived, my heart had settled into a steady rhythm of nervous anticipation. The golden light of the setting sun stretched long shadows across the camp, casting everything in a glow that felt almost unreal. I still hadn't said a word. I had waited and waited for the perfect moment, but maybe that was my mistake. Maybe perfection didn't exist. Maybe there was no *right* moment, no ideal setting. Maybe the only thing that mattered was *now*.

And then, as if the universe had heard my unspoken plea, I saw her.

She was sitting alone beneath the oak tree. *The* oak tree. The same place where I had first noticed her, where I had first felt that strange shift inside me, as if something had clicked into place. The light danced through the leaves above, painting patterns of gold and amber on her skin, and for a moment, I forgot how to breathe. She looked like something out of a dream, something too beautiful, too fleeting, too impossible to belong to the real world.

This was it.

My last chance.

I swallowed hard and forced my legs to move, each step toward her feeling heavier than the last. My hands were cold despite the warmth of the evening, my throat dry even though I hadn't spoken a single word yet. The closer I got, the louder my heartbeat became, pounding against my ribs like a war drum.

And then, finally, I was there.

She looked up as my shadow fell over her, her eyes meeting mine with the same warmth that had drawn me in from the very beginning.

"Hey," she said softly, smiling in that easy way she always did.

"Hey," I breathed, the word barely escaping my lips.

Silence.

Not an awkward silence, not an empty one, but a moment suspended in time, fragile and precious, hanging between us like something waiting to be named.

"I... I need to talk to you," I finally managed to say, my voice uneven, betraying the storm inside me.

She tilted her head slightly, curiosity flickering across her face. *"Of course,"* she said, as if she had no idea that this was the most important conversation of my life.

I inhaled deeply, steadying myself.

This was it.

I was going to tell her. I was going to say the words that had been trapped in my chest for days, the words that had kept me awake at night, that had tangled themselves in my thoughts every time I looked at her.

But just as I opened my mouth,

It happened.

A shadow appeared beside us.

I didn't even need to turn around.

I already knew who it was.

And in that instant, I felt the ground shift beneath me, as if the universe had decided to pull the moment away just as I had finally reached for it.

Sheetal's presence was like an uninvited storm, cold and unrelenting, sweeping away the fragile moment I had been holding onto. She didn't look at me, nor did she need to. Her entire stance, the way she positioned herself between us, spoke louder than words. It was a silent yet undeniable message, one that told me I was no longer part of this moment. I felt as if an invisible wall had been built in an instant, one I had no power to break.

Her voice was steady, almost casual, but there was an edge to it, a quiet insistence that left no room for argument. **"Nutan, let's go,"** she said. There was no anger, no urgency, just a calm authority that carried the weight of something unspoken.

Nutan turned to her, confused. For a second, she hesitated. Her brows furrowed, her lips parted slightly, as if she was about to protest. **"But, "** she began, and in that moment, hope flickered inside me. Perhaps she wouldn't leave just yet. Perhaps she would stay, hear me out, give me the time I so desperately needed.

But then Sheetal spoke again. This time, her voice was firmer, more resolute. **"Nutan, it's getting late."** It was not a suggestion. It was a decision.

And just like that, the moment began slipping through my fingers. I could feel it unraveling, feel the weight of missed words pressing against my chest. My heart screamed at me to act, to say something, to reach for her hand and stop her before it was too late. But my mind, my foolish, fearful mind, held me back.

I looked at Nutan, searching for something, anything, that told me she wanted to stay. And for the briefest of moments, I saw it. A hesitation. A silent question in her eyes. A pause that felt like eternity yet lasted no more than a second. She was waiting, waiting for me to give her a reason to stay. To fight for this. To fight for her.

But fear gripped me. It whispered doubts into my ears, filling my head with uncertainty. What if I was wrong? What if she was relieved that Sheetal had come? What if she had no desire to hear what I had been about to say? What if stopping her would only embarrass both of us? The what-ifs consumed me, choking my courage, making me doubt the very thing I had spent all day preparing myself for.

And then, in that hesitation, I lost her.

Nutan exhaled softly, her shoulders dropping ever so slightly, as if surrendering to an unseen force. She gave me one last glance, one that was neither regretful nor indifferent, just resigned. Then she nodded. **"Okay, let's go,"** she said, her voice quiet, almost distant.

She stood up, dusting off her hands, her movements slow but deliberate. And then, without another word, she turned away. She didn't hesitate. She didn't look back. She simply walked away, her figure blending into the night, taking with her the moment I had waited for all day.

I stood there, frozen, feeling as if something inside me had shattered. The weight of the lost opportunity pressed down on my chest, making it hard to breathe. I had been so close. So damn close. And yet, I had let my own fears steal the moment away.

That night, sleep did not come easily. I lay on my bed, staring at the ceiling, my mind replaying the evening over and over again. Each time, I imagined a different ending, one where I had spoken up, one where I had taken her hand, one where I had looked Sheetal in the eye and simply said **no, not this time.** But reality was unkind. No matter how many times I rewrote the moment in my head, the truth remained the same.

I had waited too long.

I had let hesitation win.

And now, she was gone.

The questions tormented me. What if I had just taken a step forward? What if I had called her name before she walked away? What if I had been braver, just for a few seconds more? Would she have stayed? Would she have listened? Would I have left with a heart full of hope instead of this unbearable emptiness?

I would never know.

And the worst part about lost moments is that they never truly leave you. They stay, lingering in the corners of your heart, whispering regrets, reminding you of the words left unsaid. Because sometimes, the moments you lose are the ones that haunt you forever.

EIGHT

<u>The Last Goodbye</u>

The morning of the last day felt different. The sky wasn't as blue as it had been all these days, the warm summer breeze didn't carry the same excitement, and the laughter around the campgrounds sounded distant, almost hollow. Everything felt muted, like someone had turned down the volume of life itself. Maybe it was just me. Maybe it was the weight in my chest, the aching emptiness that had taken hold ever since last night, ever since I lost my chance. The reality of it all was finally sinking in. In a few hours, this place would be gone. The friendships, the laughter, the stolen glances, the moments that had felt so infinite, they would all fade into memory. And Nutan... she would be gone, too.

I wanted to move, to go and find her, to at least say something. But my feet felt heavy, like they were rooted to the ground, as if a part of me already knew that no matter what I did, it was too late. I had spent the last fifteen days waiting, hesitating, second-guessing. And now, I had run out of time. I walked slowly toward the central courtyard, where all the campers were gathering, waiting for their parents to arrive. Some were excited, eager to go home and tell stories about their time here. Some were exchanging numbers, making promises to stay in touch. But all I could do was search for one person in the crowd. My eyes moved restlessly, scanning the familiar faces, until I saw her.

She stood near the entrance, her suitcase beside her, looking at something in the distance. She looked beautiful. The sunlight reflected in her dark hair, her soft features glowing against the golden morning. But there was something in her expression—something different. She wasn't smiling, not like she usually did. She wasn't talking to anyone. She just stood there, waiting. And I couldn't help but wonder, was she waiting for me?

But before I could take a step forward, she turned away. And that's when I saw her.

Sheetal.

Standing beside Nutan like a shadow that never left her side, her eyes scanning the crowd, watching, guarding, making sure I didn't come too close. Our eyes met for a fraction of a second, and I saw it, the final warning. The last, unspoken message between us. Don't.

And just like that, I knew.

This was the end.

The moment I had feared, the moment I had refused to accept, had arrived. Nutan was leaving. And I wasn't a part of her goodbye.

I wanted to tell myself that this didn't matter, that it was just a camp, just a summer, just a fleeting moment in the grand scheme of life. But no matter how many times I repeated those words in my head, my heart refused to believe them. This wasn't just a summer. It wasn't just a camp. And Nutan... she wasn't just some girl I met along the way. She was different.

She had become everything.

And now, she was slipping away.

I clenched my fists, my heart screaming at me to do something. To run to her, to call out her name, to make her stop, to tell her that I couldn't let this end without knowing, did she feel it, too? Did she feel that pull, that unspoken connection, that weight in the air every time we looked at each other? Or was it all just in my head? Was I the only one drowning in a storm that she had never even noticed?

I knew I wouldn't get another chance. This was my last moment. And yet, my feet stayed glued to the ground. My mind was a battlefield, one side telling me to go, to fight for what I felt, the other side whispering, It's over. You already lost her. Don't make this harder than it has to be.

And maybe, deep down, I already knew the truth. Some stories don't have happy endings. Some moments are meant to remain unfinished.

But God, it hurt.

The first car arrived, and I watched as a group of campers ran toward their parents, their voices filled with excitement, their arms wrapping around their families. The air was filled with the sounds of goodbyes, of promises to keep in touch, of laughter mixed with the bittersweet sadness of parting ways. I wondered if Nutan would remember me once she left. Would she think about me on the drive home? Would she ever go back to that rainy night, to that dance we shared, to the almost moments between us? Or would I fade into nothing, just another face in a sea of memories?

She hadn't even looked at me since she arrived at the courtyard. And maybe that was the answer.

Maybe, to her, I was already gone.

I let out a shaky breath, my fingers curling into my palms, my chest tightening with a pain I didn't know how to contain. I wasn't prepared for this. I wasn't prepared for how much it would hurt to watch her leave, to watch her world move forward while mine stood still.

And then, as if the universe had given me one last gift, she turned.

For a brief moment, our eyes met.

A second.

That's all it was.

But in that second, a thousand unspoken words passed between us.

Do you feel it, too?

Is this hurting you the way it's hurting me?

Why didn't we say something when we had the chance?

I searched her eyes, desperate for an answer. Desperate for anything.

But before I could find it, Sheetal moved.

She stepped in front of Nutan, blocking her from my sight.

And just like that, the moment was gone.

I exhaled sharply, a lump forming in my throat.

This was it.

The end of our story.

The part where she walks away.

And I stand there, watching her go, unable to do anything about it.

The world felt still, as if time itself had slowed down. Everything around me, the noise of the camp, the laughter of students saying their final goodbyes, the sound of car doors shutting, felt distant. It was as if I were standing in the middle of a storm, but instead of wind and rain, it was emotions that raged inside me. And the only thing I could focus on was her. Nutan.

She stood just a few feet away, her suitcase beside her, her back turned slightly as she hugged her friends one last time. She was leaving. And I? I was standing here like a statue, unable to move, unable to breathe, unable to do anything but watch. My heart felt like it was being ripped apart, piece by piece, with every second that passed. My chest felt tight, like someone had placed a weight on it, and no matter how hard I tried, I couldn't lift it off.

I was just 17 years old. Too young to know what real love was, they would say. Too young to understand heartbreak. But they didn't know. They didn't know what it felt like to see someone walk away, knowing you had a chance, just one chance, to change everything, but you let it slip through your fingers. They didn't know what it was like to stand there, frozen, as the person who had become the most important part of your world left without looking back.

Nutan was not just a girl I met in summer camp. She was the first person who made my heart race, the first person who made me feel like I was more than just a boy from a small town. She was the first dream that had ever felt real. And now, she was slipping away.

Her parents had arrived a few minutes ago. I had watched them greet her, had seen the way she smiled at them, a smile that once felt like it belonged to me, but now, I realized, it never really did. I wanted to move, to step forward, to call her name. But I didn't. My body refused to listen to my heart. And maybe, just maybe, it was because I was afraid of what would happen if I did.

What if I stopped her, and she looked at me with empty eyes, with no feeling at all? What if she laughed softly and said, "Sunil, it was just camp. It was fun, but it's over now." What if I held onto something that had never even been mine?

So I stood still.

Even as she hugged Sheetal. Even as she lifted her suitcase. Even as she turned toward the car.

I stood there, watching, waiting, hoping, praying, that she would turn one last time. That she would glance over her shoulder and give me something, anything to hold on to.

But she didn't.

She walked to the car, her movements slow, unhurried, like she had all the time in the world. But for me? Time was running out.

And then it happened.

She reached the car door.

Paused.

And for one second, she turned.

Her eyes found mine.

And in that second, the world collapsed around me.

I don't know what I was expecting. Maybe I wanted her to smile, to silently tell me that she would miss me too, that she wished things had been different. Maybe I wanted her to nod, as if saying, "I know what you feel, Sunil. I feel it too."

But she did none of that.

She just looked at me.

And her eyes... they weren't empty.

They were full of something I couldn't understand.

A sadness, maybe. A quiet longing. Or perhaps, it was just my imagination—a foolish 17-year-old boy, seeing what he wanted to see instead of the truth.

Because before I could figure it out, before I could move, before I could do anything, she turned away.

She got into the car.

The door closed.

The engine started.

And my heart?

It shattered into pieces.

I wanted to run to her. I wanted to scream her name. I wanted to pound on the car window and beg her to stay, to listen, to let me say the words I had been too afraid to speak.

But I didn't.

Because what would be the point?

She had made her choice.

And I... I had lost.

So I did the only thing I could.

I stood there, watching, letting the pain tear me apart from the inside.

As the car began to roll forward, as the distance between us grew, my hands clenched into fists. My nails dug into my skin, but I barely felt it. My throat burned, but I swallowed the lump that had formed there. My eyes stung, but I refused to let the tears fall.

Because boys don't cry, right? That's what they always say.

But at that moment, I wasn't a boy.

I was just a heartbroken 17-year-old, watching the first person he had ever cared about disappear from his life forever.

The car was almost at the gate now. And still, she didn't look back. Still, she didn't stop.

Still, she kept moving, taking a part of me with her.

I thought about everything we had shared, the dance in the rain, the stolen glances, the moments of silence that spoke louder than words. I thought about how she had smiled at me, how she had sung that song that felt like it was meant for me.

And I realized something.

Maybe she did feel something too.

Maybe, deep down, she had known.

Maybe she had wanted to say something just as much as I had.

But like me, she had been afraid.

Afraid of what would happen if she admitted it.

Afraid of what would come next.

Afraid of ruining something that was never meant to last.

Maybe... she was just as broken as I was.

The car reached the main road. Turned the corner. And just like that, she was gone. Gone, like she had never been here at all. Gone, leaving behind only memories and an unbearable emptiness.

And I? I was left standing in the middle of the camp, surrounded by people, yet feeling completely and utterly alone.

The world didn't stop. The sun didn't stop shining. People kept talking, kept laughing, kept moving forward. But I?

I was stuck.

Stuck in that moment.

Stuck in the what-ifs.

What if I had spoken sooner?

What if I had told her how I felt?

What if I had stopped her from leaving?

Would anything have changed?

Would she have stayed?

Would she have been mine?

I would never know.

And that was the worst part.

Because sometimes, the moments you don't take...

Are the ones that haunt you forever.

NINE

<u>Some Melodies Never End</u>

Time passed.

The seasons changed, the years moved forward, and life continued like it always does. But some things never change. Some loves never truly leave you. They become a quiet ache, a whisper in the back of your mind, a shadow that lingers even when you think you've outrun it. And Nutan was mine.

She was no longer in my life, but she was everywhere.

In the songs that played on the radio, in the way the rain smelled before a storm, in the laughter of a girl passing by. Sometimes, I would hear someone call her name in a crowd, and my heart would stop for a second, my body turning before my mind reminded me, it wasn't her.

But for that single second, it always felt like she had come back.

Even as I grew older, even as my world changed, the summer we spent together never lost its place in my heart. It remained frozen in time, untouched by everything else. I tried to tell myself that it was just a teenage dream, that first loves are always supposed to be unforgettable because they are our first taste of something beyond friendship, beyond innocence. But no matter how much I reasoned with myself, it never felt that simple.

Because some moments don't fade.

Some names stay etched in your soul forever.

And some melodies never end.

I tried to move on. I really did. But forgetting isn't something you can force. You don't wake up one day and decide, Today, I will forget. Because memories aren't stored in places you can control. They live in smells, in sounds, in unexpected moments that pull you back without warning.

I would be walking down the street, lost in thought, and suddenly the scent of wet earth after a rainstorm would hit me, and just like that, I would be back in that summer. I would see her twirling in the rain, hear the sound of her laughter mixing with the storm, feel the warmth of her hand brushing against mine. It never went away. I fell in love again, or at least, I tried to.

I met other girls. I dated. I told myself that this is what moving on looks like. I convinced myself that love isn't meant to last forever, that sometimes, the best thing you can do is let go. And yet, every time I got close to someone, something held me back.

I didn't mean to compare them to her. I didn't want to. But deep inside, I knew. I would never love anyone the way I loved her. Because first love is different. It is raw, it is pure, and most of all, it is unfinished.

It doesn't come with a clean ending. It leaves behind pieces of itself, places inside you that no one else can reach. And when you close your eyes at night, when everything else is silent, it is the only thing you hear.

Because some melodies never end.

Years passed, and I grew older. I built a life for myself, a career, friendships, responsibilities. My world expanded, but she remained a part of it, tucked away in a quiet corner of my heart, untouched by time. Sometimes, I wondered if I would ever meet her again. Would fate ever be kind enough to give me one last moment with her?

Not to change the past, not to rewrite our story, but just to see her one last time, to know that she was happy, to hear her voice once more, to know that our memories were not mine alone to carry. But life doesn't always give you closure. Some questions remain unanswered. Some love stories are never meant to have a reunion. And so, I let the days pass, carrying her memory with me like a song that played softly in the background of my life.

People say first love teaches you more than any other. And maybe that's true. Because even though Nutan was no longer in my life, she shaped the person I became. She taught me that love isn't just about what is said, it's about what is felt, what is left unsaid, what lingers even when everything else is gone. She taught me that some things don't need to be spoken to be real. That sometimes, the most powerful love stories are the ones that remain unfinished. And most of all, she taught me that love doesn't always mean staying together.

Sometimes, love means letting go.

Even when it hurts.

Even when it feels impossible.

Even when it stays with you forever.

Because some melodies never end.

There were nights , many nights.... when I lay awake, staring at the ceiling, wondering if she ever thought of me too.

Did she ever hear a song and remember me?

Did she ever feel the rain and think of that night when we danced?

Did she ever stop, just for a second, and wonder where I was, what I was doing, if I had moved on?

Or was I just a distant memory, a summer that faded into her past without leaving a trace?

I would never know. And maybe that was the saddest part of all.

Life doesn't wait for you. No matter how much you want to hold on to a moment, time pulls you forward, I left Goa, shifted to Mumbai. I travelled. I met new people. I built a life that was full, a life that had meaning. But no matter how much time passed, one thing remained the same. She was the love that shaped me. The one who taught me that some feelings never fade, no matter how much time passes. And even though I never saw her again, even though she became just a memory, she was never just a memory to me.

She was my first love.

My greatest what-if.

The melody that would always play in the background of my life. Because some songs don't need an ending. They just need to be heard. And some melodies never end.

This is not just a love story.

It is a story about growing up, about accepting the past, about learning that not every love is meant to last forever, but that doesn't make it any less real.

Sunil and Nutan's love were unfinished, but unforgettable. And sometimes, the most beautiful love stories are the ones that remain open-ended, lingering in our hearts like a song that never truly stops playing.

Because some melodies never end....

TEN

Mumbai – July 2007

The train pulled into Chhatrapati Shivaji Terminal (CST) at dawn, the grand Gothic structure standing tall like a guardian of history, its intricate architecture whispering tales of a time long past. The first golden rays of the sun stretched across the sky, casting a warm glow over the city that had already been awake for hours. Mumbai didn't wake up with the sun.... it never slept.

As I stepped off the train, I was immediately swallowed by the crowd, my suitcase clutched tightly in my hands. It was as if I had entered a living, breathing organism, where every person moved with purpose, rushing forward like waves in an unstoppable tide. There was a strange energy in the air, chaotic yet alive, suffocating yet thrilling. This was Mumbai the city of dreams, the city that consumed people whole, the city that either made you or broke you.

I had only seen Mumbai in Bollywood movies, its dazzling skyline and Marine Drive's sparkling waves romanticized in slow-motion shots. But standing here now, amidst the honking taxis, screaming vendors, and impatient commuters, I realized that Mumbai wasn't just a city. It was an emotion.

It didn't take long for me to realize that in Mumbai, if you couldn't keep up, you'd be left behind.

I had barely taken in my surroundings when I was shoved forward, pushed into a line of passengers scrambling to board the Mumbai local train, the lifeline of the city. I had heard stories about the legendary local trains, where getting inside during rush hour was nothing short of a battle. But experiencing it firsthand? That was an entirely different reality.

As the train arrived at the platform, hundreds of people surged forward, pushing, shoving, climbing over each other, desperate to grab a foothold. It didn't matter if the train was already packed there was always room for one more, even if it meant hanging from the edge, one foot in the air.

I hesitated for a second, and in that second, five people had already taken the space in front of me.

"This is it, Sunil," I muttered to myself. "This is your Mumbai initiation."

Summoning every ounce of courage, I lunged forward, squeezing into a tiny gap between two men who smelled of sweat and cheap aftershave. Someone's elbow was digging into my ribs, someone else's bag was pressed against my back, and the sheer heat of human bodies packed together made it almost impossible to breathe.

But as the train started moving, I felt something shift. The rhythm of the city, the pulse of the crowd, the heartbeat of Mumbai, it consumed me.

I was now one of them.

As the train raced past the endless slums, towering skyscrapers, and billboards advertising everything from Bollywood movies to fairness creams, I couldn't help but think about Goa. Mumbai and Goa were like two different worlds, two different lives.

In Goa, time moved slowly. The mornings were calm, the streets lined with palm trees swaying in the breeze. The air smelled of salt and coconuts, and the only sounds were the distant crashing of waves and the occasional honk of a sleepy motorcyclist.

But in Mumbai, time ran. There was no breeze, only the thick humidity that clung to your skin. The air smelled of exhaust fumes, frying vada pav, and the dampness of unwashed bodies squeezed together in trains.

Back home, I could walk barefoot on the soft, golden sands of Miramar Beach and feel the water lap at my toes. Here, the Arabian Sea was known to me, yet foreign. The sea in Mumbai wasn't a place for relaxation it was a place for dreams, heartbreaks, and stolen moments.

In Goa, I had spent carefree evenings riding my bicycle through quiet streets, the sun setting in hues of orange and pink. In Mumbai, the sun disappeared behind tall buildings, swallowed by the skyline long before it could touch the ground.

Goa was a lazy Sunday morning.

Mumbai was a Monday rush-hour that never ended.

And I?

I was a Goan boy thrown into the madness of Mumbai, trying to find my place in this city of endless movement.

By the time I reached Belapur, exhausted and drenched in sweat, my stomach was growling. I had survived my first Mumbai local ride, but I was now faced with another challenge, Mumbai Street food.

I spotted a vada pav stall near the CBD station, its golden-fried potato patties sizzling in a giant pan of oil. The vendor worked like an artist, slathering the pav with spicy chutney, stuffing in the crisp vada, and handing it over in a piece of old newspaper.

I took a bite—and instantly, I knew.

This was Mumbai.

The heat of the chilies, the crunch of the batter, the softness of the pav, it was a city packed into a single bite. Spicy, fast, overwhelming, and yet, something about it made you want more. A steaming glass of cutting chai arrived next. The strong, sweet tea mixed with ginger and cardamom burned my throat, but it also revived my senses.

I leaned against the wall, watching the people around me, students rushing to college, office workers checking their phones, rickshaw drivers haggling with passengers.

I had been in Mumbai for only a few hours, but I already understood one thing.

This city didn't stop for anyone. If I wanted to survive here, I had to become a part of its rhythm.

As I finally reached Bharati Vidyapeeth College in CBD Belapur, I stood in front of the massive gates, taking a deep breath. This was the beginning of my new life. I was here to become a hotel management student, to build a future in the world of luxury and hospitality. But deep inside, I knew the truth. I hadn't just come here for my career. I had come here to escape.

To drown myself in studies, work, and the never-ending rush of Mumbai. Mumbai doesn't welcome you with open arms it challenges you, dares you, tests your patience, and if you survive, it makes you its own. In those early days of my college life, I didn't just live in Mumbai, I was consumed by it.

The city had a heartbeat, a pulse that never slowed down. There was no space for weakness, no room for hesitation. Mumbai demanded everything from you, your time, your energy, your soul.

Every morning, I was thrown into the madness of local trains. It didn't matter if I was tired, if my body ached from the previous day, if I needed a moment to breathe, the train had no mercy. The battle began as soon as I reached the station. The hustle, the crowd, the smell of sweat and the ocean breeze mixing in the air, everything about it screamed chaos. The doors would open, and it was war.

People pushed, shoved, elbowed their way in. If you weren't quick enough, you'd be left behind, and in Mumbai, being left behind was not an option. I learned how to move with the crowd, how to jump onto a moving train, how to stand my ground even when I was squeezed between a dozen strangers, my backpack pressed against my chest.

Inside the compartment, there was no space for personal boundaries. The man next to me would have his arm digging into my side, someone else's bag would be hitting my shoulder, and if I was lucky enough to get a seat, my legs would ache from keeping them folded to make space for others.

Yet, somehow, it became normal.

The rhythm of the city seeped into my bones. The sounds, the distant honking, the rhythmic clatter of the train on the tracks, the chaiwalas shouting at the station, it all became a part of me. I wasn't just in Mumbai anymore. Mumbai was in me.

At Bharati Vidyapeeth College of Hotel Management, there was no time to slow down. Mornings began with kitchen training, where we learned how to hold a knife properly, how to dice onions without crying, how to stir a sauce without burning it. The kitchen was a battlefield, and we were expected to be soldiers of perfection.

"You are not just cooking," our instructor reminded us daily. "You are creating an experience."

We learned to fold napkins into intricate designs, to balance trays like professionals, to pour wine with elegance. Hospitality was an art, and we were being trained to master it. But beyond the lessons in fine dining and customer service, there was the real struggle of being a student in Mumbai.

We didn't just study, we survived.

Many days, there was no time for a proper meal. I'd grab a vada pav from a street vendor, burn my tongue on the spicy chutney, wash it down with cutting chai, and rush to my next class. the time evening arrived; exhaustion clung to me like a second skin. My body ached from standing for hours in the kitchen, from running between classes, from constantly being on my feet.

But the day wasn't over.

Many students, including me, took part-time jobs at hotels, working as interns, waiters, or receptionists just to earn extra money and gain experience.

Some nights, I wouldn't reach my hostel until midnight, my uniform still smelling like spices, my shoes coated in dust from the streets. Yet, even as I collapsed onto my bed, there was a sense of satisfaction. I was becoming something. I was shaping a future, carving out a name for myself.

I was growing.

If Mumbai's streets were a battlefield, then hostel life was the survival camp. The small, cramped rooms felt like a box with barely enough air to breathe. Three of us were stuffed into a space meant for two. The beds were hard, the walls thin, and the fans creaked so loudly at night that they could drive a person mad.

There was no privacy, no peace.

One guy would be talking on the phone late into the night, another snoring loudly in his sleep, and outside, the constant sound of honking and distant conversations never really stopped.

Showers? A luxury. You had to wake up before sunrise if you wanted hot water. If you were late, you were left with ice-cold punishment.

The mess food was a gamble, some nights, dal and rice were edible. Other nights, it felt like I was chewing flavoured water. We learned to survive on street food, and vada pav became my daily staple.

But the best part of hostel life?

The friendships.

We were all struggling together. We shared everything, food, laughter, late-night conversations about dreams we weren't sure we could ever achieve. On weekends, we'd escape to Marine Drive, sit by the sea, watch the city lights reflect on the Arabian waters, and talk about life, love, and the future that felt so far away.

No matter how much Mumbai distracted me, challenged me, pushed me forward, one thing never changed.

The ache inside me.

At night, when the city finally grew quiet, when the hostel lights dimmed, when the sounds of laughter and arguments faded, my mind would always return to one name.

Nutan.

She was a ghost that lived inside me, a shadow that followed me through the bustling crowds, a whisper in the back of my mind even when I was laughing with my friends.

Where was she?

Did she ever think of me?

Had she forgotten?

I tried to push these thoughts away. I told myself it had been four years. People moved on. People forgot.

But I couldn't.

No matter how much I tried, she was still there, in the unspoken spaces of my life.

The City That Made You, and the City That Broke You, Mumbai was a city of contrasts. It gave you hope, but it also gave you loneliness. It made you, but it also broke you. I was learning to survive, learning to belong, learning to keep moving forward. But inside me, something remained unfinished.

Some wounds don't heal. Some memories don't fade. Some names never leave you.

And Nutan was one of them.

In a city of millions, how does one feel alone? This city was a symphony of chaos, an orchestra where every instrument played its own tune, and yet, somehow, the music never stopped. It was a place where dreams were built and broken in the same breath, where people walked side by side yet never truly saw each other.

Everywhere I looked, there were people, rushing, running, pushing past one another, chasing something unseen. They lived in apartments stacked like puzzle pieces, their lives separated by thin walls, their hearts separated by something even thinner indifference.

I had never seen a place so full of people, yet so empty of connection.

There were mornings when I walked through the streets of Vashi, past vendors selling fresh flowers and newspaper boys yelling the headlines, past chai stalls crowded with men discussing cricket and politics, and still, I felt like a ghost drifting through it all. At Marine Drive, couples sat close, their fingers entwined, whispering secrets only the waves could hear. At Juhu Beach, lovers carved names into the sand, only for the sea to take them away moments later, as if reminding them that nothing lasts forever.

Even in the suffocating compartments of local trains, love found a way. A young man would glance at a girl across the aisle, their eyes meeting for a fleeting second before she turned away, a shy smile betraying her indifference. An old couple sat together, the man's fingers tracing the wrinkles on his wife's hands, a lifetime of love spoken in silence.

Mumbai was a city that believed in love.

And yet, I had never felt more distant from it. I should have been happy for them, the strangers who found comfort in each other, the lovers who laughed under the city lights, the hands that held on tight in a world that was always slipping away.

But instead, I was jealous.

I wished Nutan was sitting beside me at Marine Drive, her head resting on my shoulder as the waves kissed the shore. I wished I could turn in a crowded street and find her smiling at me, the way she used to, when we were sixteen and the world felt full of possibilities. But Mumbai had no traces of her.

She was gone. Just like the summer we spent together. Just like the words I never had the courage to say.

They say time heals everything. That if you keep moving forward, the past will eventually stop chasing you. But that's not true. Because some memories don't fade. Some wounds never close. Some names never leave your lips, even when you stop speaking to them out loud. Nutan was a shadow in my life, a presence that never left, yet was never there.

Some nights, I would dream of her. I would wake up, heart pounding, reaching out for someone who wasn't there. The taste of her name lingered on my tongue, but the more I tried to hold onto the dream, the faster it slipped through my fingers, just like she had.

This city was a city that never waited, but I still found myself waiting, for something, for someone, for a moment that would never come. There were nights when I walked alone through Colaba, past the yellow lights of Leopold Café, past the street musicians playing old Hindi songs, past the bookstores filled with stories of love and loss. And in every corner of the city, I searched for her.

In the eyes of strangers, in the laughter of passing girls, in the reflection of the sea at Marine Drive, I searched for her as if she had left clues behind, as if fate had hidden her somewhere just beyond my reach.

But fate was silent.

And so was she.

This city was loud, but my loneliness was louder.

I had friends, I had classmates, roommates, people to share my time with. But none of them knew the truth. None of them knew that every night, when I laid down on my hostel bed, staring at the cracked ceiling, I wasn't in Mumbai anymore. I was sixteen again, standing in a rain-soaked field, watching Nutan spin in circles with her arms wide open. I was back in the summer that changed everything. And I was stuck there, trapped in a story that had no ending.

Some Love Stories Don't End, They Just Pause

One evening, I found myself back at Marine Drive. The sky had turned a deep shade of blue, the first stars flickering above the city skyline. People around me talked, laughed, held hands, shared stolen kisses under the dim streetlights.

And I sat there, alone, watching the waves crash against the rocks.

I pulled out my phone, staring at the black screen. I could have called someone. I could have messaged a friend. I could have reached out to anyone. But there was only one name I wanted to type. And I had no number, no way to reach her, no idea where she was in this vast world.

So, I sat there, in the city that never slept, in the place where dreams were made and broken and I let myself feel the weight of missing her.

The year 2007 wasn't just another passing year, it was the year India truly stepped into the digital world. The internet had arrived, and it was changing everything. Social media wasn't just an option anymore; it was a revolution.

From Orkut to Yahoo Messenger, from Google searches to the earliest days of Facebook, people weren't just living their real lives, they were building parallel digital identities. This was the first time that memories, friendships, and even love could exist in a world beyond physical space. The whole country was suddenly obsessed with this new way of connecting. Everyone wanted to search for someone, a childhood best friend, a college crush, a lost family member, or just someone they had met once and never saw again. It was a time when people weren't just looking forward; they were looking back.

In college, having an Orkut account wasn't a choice, it was a necessity. If you weren't on Orkut, you didn't exist. Boys spent hours scraping on each other's profiles, joining random communities, and sending friend requests to girls they had never even spoken to in real life. Girls, on the other hand, carefully curated their profiles, choosing the perfect profile picture, status updates, and testimonials from friends. It was an addiction. The first thing people did in the morning was check their Orkut profile. The last thing they did before going to bed was refresh their messages. But for me, Orkut wasn't about making new friends. It was about finding an old one. The Gateway to the Past

From the day I stepped into Mumbai, I created my Orkut profile not to connect with strangers, but to search for one name, Nutan. Every night, after a long and exhausting day of college, kitchen training, and hostel life, I would find myself at a small, dimly lit cyber café near my hostel, staring at the bright blue glow of the Orkut homepage. The search bar became my obsession.

Nutan.

I typed her name and pressed enter. Hundreds of Nutans appeared. None of them were her.

I tried different spellings. Nutan thakare, Nutan Thakre, Nootan ....

Nothing.

I clicked on profiles, my heart racing each time a familiar-looking face loaded on the screen. But it was never her.

Had she changed her name? Had she deleted her profile? Or worse... had she forgotten me completely? With every failed search, my hope started to crack.

Orkut was a place for reconnecting lost souls, but maybe, I was the only one searching. Maybe she had already moved on. Maybe I was just a boy stuck in the past, holding onto memories that had faded long ago.

But even then, even after endless nights of dead ends, I wasn't ready to give up.

Not yet.

Because somewhere in the vastness of this digital universe, I still believed she was out there. People spent their entire lives trying to make it big, trying to rise above the millions who walked the same streets, breathed the same air, and dreamed the same dreams. Some succeeded, most failed. And some, like me, were just searching for something they had lost along the way.

ELEVEN

<u>One Night. One Notification. Everything Changed.</u>

It was a Tuesday night when it happened. Like every other night, I had logged in with no real hope, just the same old habit of searching. But this time, something was different. The moment I landed on my homepage, I saw it. A small red notification at the top of the screen.

"Profile Visitors: 1 New."

My heart skipped a beat.

Who would visit my profile?

I wasn't popular on Orkut. I barely posted. I barely interacted. With shaking hands, I clicked on the notification. And my breath stopped.

Sheetal Deshmukh.

The moment I saw her name; my hands froze over the keyboard. A name I hadn't thought about in years. A name that carried the weight of a thousand unanswered questions.

For a few seconds, I just stared at the screen, my heart hammering against my ribs. The small notification on my Orkut page seemed to glow brighter than anything else in the dim cyber café.

Why had she visited my profile?

It wasn't just curiosity. Sheetal and I had never been friends. If anything, she had always been a wall between

Nutan and me. And yet, here she was searching for me after four long years.

Was this a coincidence?

Or was it something more?

I swallowed hard, my fingers hovering over the keyboard. Should I send her a message? Should I wait for her to reach out? Should I ignore it? I took a deep breath, my mind racing through every memory I had of her. Sheetal had always been the silent protector, Nutan's shadow. She had watched me with careful eyes during summer camp, always suspicious of my presence around Nutan.

Back then, I had assumed she just didn't like me.

But now, as I sat in this dimly lit cyber café, staring at her name on my screen, a thought hit me like a cold wave. Had she been protecting Nutan from me... or from something else?

My hands trembled as I clicked on her profile. Her profile picture was blurry, taken on a phone camera, but she looked the same. The same sharp eyes. The same confident expression.

Her bio read: "Aviation Student. Dreamer. Too busy for nonsense." ☹

Typical Sheetal.

I scrolled through her profile, searching for any clues about Nutan. Her friend list was locked, her scraps were filled with random conversations, and her testimonials were from college friends.

Nothing.

No mention of Nutan. No photos. No posts that could give me even the faintest clue. But then again, why would she visit my profile if she didn't remember our past? I leaned back in my chair, staring at the flickering computer screen. For weeks, I had searched for Nutan with no success. And now, out of nowhere, her best friend had appeared like a ghost from my past.

Was this fate?

Or was this just another false hope that would leave me broken all over again?

I closed my eyes, breathing deeply.

If I reached out to Sheetal, there were only two possibilities.

One: She would ignore me.

Two: She would tell me something I wasn't ready to hear.

Either way, I had to know.

I couldn't keep running in circles. I had spent years haunted by Nutan's memory, searching for her shadow in every face I passed. If Sheetal knew something, anything, I needed to hear it.

With a pounding heart, I clicked on the "Send Friend Request" button. The request was sent.

Now, all I could do was wait.

The minutes stretched into hours.

The cyber café buzzed around me, students chatting over Yahoo Messenger, boys looking up cricket scores, a couple sitting in the corner giggling as they shared a single pair of earphones. But I was trapped in my own world, my eyes fixed on the pending friend request notification. Every few minutes, I refreshed the page.

Nothing.

No acceptance. No message. No sign that she had even noticed.

I ran a hand through my hair, frustrated. Had she visited my profile by accident? Maybe she had searched for an old friend and clicked on me by mistake?

No.

Sheetal was too sharp for that. She never did anything without a reason.

But if she had a reason... why wasn't she responding?

My fingers drummed against the keyboard. The urge to send her a scrap, to type out "Hey, remember me?" burned inside me. But something held me back. I had to be patient. If she had searched for me, she would know I had seen it. She would know I had sent a request. Now, it was her turn to make a move.

With a sigh, I logged out. The screen flickered black as I pushed my chair back.

Outside, the city was alive with its usual chaos. The smell of street food filled the air, rickshaws honked impatiently, and a Bollywood song played from a nearby stall. I walked aimlessly, my mind still trapped in Orkut, in summer camp, in Nutan's smile, in Sheetal's cold stare.

That night, sleep refused to come. Every time I closed my eyes, my mind filled with questions, looping endlessly like a broken record.

Where was Nutan?

Why had Sheetal searched for me?

Would she accept my request?

Would she tell me something I wasn't ready to hear?

I tossed and turned in my small hostel bed, the room around me silent except for the slow, whirring fan above. My roommate, Ashutosh, was snoring softly, completely unaware of the storm raging inside me. The glow of the streetlights outside cast faint shadows on the walls, but nothing could distract me from the anticipation tightening in my chest.

At 2 AM, I couldn't take it anymore. I reached for my laptop, the screen glowing too bright in the darkness. My fingers moved on instinct, opening the Orkut.com.

And then—I saw it. A red notification blinked at the top of the screen. "Friend Request Accepted – Sheetal Deshmukh." My breath caught in my throat.

She had accepted.

For a moment, I just stared at the screen, my heart pounding like a war drum. After weeks of searching, after months of longing, after four years of silence, the past had finally come knocking. My hand trembled as I clicked on her profile. Before I could process what I was seeing, another notification popped up.

"New Scrap from Sheetal Deshmukh."

A message.

I swallowed hard, my fingers hovering over the screen. A thousand emotions surged through me, excitement, fear, longing, and something dangerously close to hope. Taking a deep breath, I clicked on it. The words appeared before me, simple yet powerful.

"Hey Sunil. Itzz been a long tym. Hw R U?"

For a moment, I just stared at the message, my brain struggling to process the simplicity of it. She wasn't talking about Nutan. She wasn't asking about the past. She was just asking about me. And somehow, that hurt more than anything else.

But instead, it was just a casual greeting, like we were old classmates catching up. Like she hadn't been the one person standing between me and Nutan all those years ago. Like she hadn't avoided my friend request for months before suddenly appearing out of nowhere. I reread the message over and over, my fingers itching to type a reply.

I could ask her straight away.

I could demand answers.

I could tell her I wasn't here for small talk; I wanted to know about Nutan.

But something stopped me.

What if she really didn't want to talk about it?

What if she was just being polite, testing the waters, seeing if I still remembered her?

What if this was the only chance I had to get any information, and if I pushed too hard, she would disappear again?

I let out a slow breath, my hands tightening around the phone.

No.

I couldn't rush this.

If Sheetal had searched for me, if she had accepted my request, then there was a reason.

I just had to be patient. So, instead of throwing all my questions at her, I typed out a reply. "Hey, Sheetal! Yeah, it's been forever. I'm good. Just busy with college and work. What about you?"

I hit send before I could second-guess myself.

Then, I waited.

Minutes passed.

Then ten minutes.

Then fifteen.

I checked my computer again, my eyes scanning for a reply.

Nothing.

The cyber café felt too small, the air too suffocating. I felt trapped, my thoughts spiraling.

Had I said something wrong?

Had she changed her mind about talking to me?

Or was she just as uncertain about this conversation as I was?

The questions gnawed at me, but there was nothing I could do except wait.

At 10 AM, still nothing. By afternoon, frustration gnawed at my patience. Had she changed her mind? Had she only accepted my request out of curiosity, then decided I wasn't worth responding to?

I felt like I was back to square one, chasing ghosts, searching for people who didn't want to be found.

The hours stretched endlessly, each second heavier than the last.

Then, finally

At 4:37 PM, a notification popped up.

"New Scrap from Sheetal Deshmukh."

My heart leapt into my throat. I opened it instantly, my eyes scanning the words like a starving man searching for food.

"I'm good too, Sunil. Life has been busy. I'm in Mumbai now, studying aviation at Frankfinn Institute. What about you?"

Mumbai.

She was here. In the same city. Just a few kilometres away. The realization hit me like a truck. I had spent years searching for Nutan, assuming she was somewhere far away, in another city, living another life. But now, the first person who could give me answers was right here. Closer than I had ever expected. And suddenly, for the first time in years, I felt like I was getting somewhere.

-

The possibilities swirled in my mind. If Sheetal was in Mumbai, if we met in person, would she finally tell me something about Nutan? would she break the silence that had lasted four years? or was this just another dead end, another cruel joke played by fate? I wasn't sure. But I knew one thing, I had to see her.

I had to look into her eyes and find out why she had searched for me. And, more than anything, I had to find out if she still carried Nutan's shadow in her heart the way I did in mine. I took a deep breath, my fingers hovering over the keyboard. Then, I typed the words that would change everything.

"That's great, Sheetal. We should meet up sometime." And then, with a racing heart, I hit send.

Now, all I could do was wait for her answer.

Because this wasn't just about Sheetal. This was about the past. The truth. The one person I had spent four years searching for. This was about Nutan.

She Replied – yes Lets meet, Raghuleela Mall ???

TWELVE

<u>The Face of the Past</u>

The days leading up to the meeting with Sheetal felt like they stretched endlessly. No matter how much I tried to keep myself occupied, my thoughts kept circling back to the same questions. Why had she searched for me? what did she know about Nutan? was she going to tell me something that would change my life forever?

Even though I had imagined meeting Sheetal so many times before, now that it was finally happening, I wasn't sure how I felt about it. There was a strange nervous energy in my chest, a mix of excitement and dread.

The thought of seeing Sheetal again after four years made me feel as though I was standing on the edge of a cliff. The past was behind me, the unknown was ahead, and I had no choice but to take the leap.

I barely slept the night before. My mind was restless, caught in the whirlwind of memories from our summer camp. The last time I had seen Sheetal, she was walking beside Nutan, pulling her away from me. She had been my biggest obstacle back then, the silent wall that stood between me and Nutan.

And now?

Now, she was the only bridge I had left to Nutan.

The irony of it all wasn't lost on me.

The sun was setting when I rode toward RaghuLeela Mall in Vashi. The Mumbai streets were alive with their usual chaos, endless honking, pedestrians weaving through traffic like it was an obstacle course, and street vendors shouting out their prices. The city smelled of spicy street food, freshly brewed chai, and petrol fumes, a strange, intoxicating mix that felt like home now. But today, I barely noticed any of it.

Today, my world was reduced to just one destination. But there was something else about today, something that made me feel a little different. Today, I was on a Pulsar 150, a sleek, powerful machine that wasn't mine. I had borrowed it from my friend Ashutosh Kulkarni.

Ashutosh was the kind of guy who never asked too many questions. When I told him I had an important meeting with a girl, he just grinned and tossed me his bike keys.

"Impress her, bro," he had said, winking.

I didn't correct him.

I didn't tell him that this wasn't about impressing a girl.

This was about finding answers.

Still, when I revved the engine and felt the power beneath me, I couldn't help but smile. Maybe a little confidence wouldn't hurt.

I had thought about this moment for so long, imagined it a thousand times in my head, but now that it was happening, I wasn't sure how to take the first step. Would she greet me with a smile? Would she be cold and distant? Would she say something that would change everything?

Taking a deep breath, I finally walked towards her.

As if sensing my presence, she looked up. Our eyes met. And just like that, the four years that had passed vanished into nothing. There was recognition in her gaze, a flicker of something deep, something unspoken. She tilted her head slightly, almost like she was trying to figure out if the boy from summer camp was really standing before her.

For the first time in a long time, I felt like I was standing in the past and the present at the same time.

She didn't smile.

But she didn't look away either.

Instead, she simply nodded, her expression unreadable.

"Sunil," she said, her voice softer than I remembered.

"Sheetal," I replied, pulling out the chair across from her.

As I sat down, I realized that my hands were shaking slightly.

I clenched them under the table, forcing myself to stay calm.

She studied me for a moment, and then, finally, a small smile played on her lips.

"You look different," she said. "More... grown-up."

I chuckled, leaning back. "Well, four years do that to a person."

She nodded but didn't respond.

For a few moments, we just sat there. Two people who had once known each other, who had once shared the same space, but now felt like strangers trying to bridge a gap that time had widened. I wanted to ask about Nutan immediately, but something about her body language told me to wait.

She wasn't here to play games.

She had searched for me.

She had accepted my request.

She had something to say.

I just had to wait for her to say it.

The conversation started slow, almost hesitant.

We talked about Mumbai, college, careers. She told me about her aviation course at Frankfinn Institute in Bandra.

I told her about my hotel management studies at Bharati Vidyapeeth in Belapur.

She mentioned how she had come to Mumbai alone, how she had to fight her way through the chaos of the city.

I told her I knew exactly how that felt.

For the first time, we weren't rivals.

We weren't fighting over Nutan's attention.

We were just two people catching up after four years.

But despite the ease of our conversation, there was a tension beneath it all.

I could feel it.

She could feel it.

We were dancing around the real reason we were here.

Finally, after a long pause, I couldn't take it anymore.

I leaned forward slightly, lowering my voice.

"Sheetal."

She looked up, her fingers stopping their gentle tapping on the table.

"There's something I need to ask you," I said.

Her body stiffened.

For the first time, I saw something flash in her eyes, fear? hesitation? regret?

But she didn't look away.

She waited.

I took a deep breath.

Then, I said the one name that had been hanging between us all evening.

"Nutan."

The moment I said it, I saw it.

A flicker of pain.

A ghost of a memory.

And just like that, I knew.

This wasn't just a meeting.

This wasn't just a coincidence.

Sheetal had been waiting for this moment too. She had been waiting to tell me something. Something that would change everything. The moment I said Nutan's name, it was as if the air between us changed. The sound of her name still felt sacred, as if it carried the weight of something unfinished, something fragile. Sheetal's fingers tightened around the coffee cup in front of her. She didn't speak. She didn't move. She just stared at the table, as if trying to find the right words in the swirls of the leftover foam.

The silence stretched between us, thick and suffocating.

I felt my own heartbeat pounding in my ears, waiting, hoping, that she would finally say something that would bring me closer to the truth I had been chasing for years. Finally, after what felt like an eternity, she took a slow breath and looked up.

Her eyes held something I couldn't quite place, regret? Pain? Or was it something else entirely?

"Sunil..." she began, her voice softer than before. "Why are you still looking for her?"

The question hit me harder than I expected.

I had been so focused on asking about Nutan, on demanding answers, that I had never stopped to think about what my search really meant. Why was I still looking for Nutan? the truth was, I didn't even know anymore. Maybe I wanted closure. Maybe I wanted to see if she still remembered me. Maybe... deep down, I was still hoping that fate would bring us back together. But I didn't say any of that. Instead, I swallowed hard and said, "Because I never got to say goodbye."

Sheetal exhaled slowly, looking out of the café window.

Outside, the world continued like nothing had changed. Couples walked hand in hand. Friends laughed. Life moved on. But inside this small space, time had stopped. She turned back to me, her expression unreadable.

"I never understood you," she said. "Back at the camp, I used to think you were just another boy who had a crush on my best friend."

She paused, her fingers playing with the edge of her napkin.

"But then I saw you watching her. The way you looked at her when she wasn't looking. The way you held your breath every time she smiled. It wasn't just a crush, was it?"

I shook my head. "No. It wasn't."

She sighed. "I know."

A flicker of something flashed in her eyes before she quickly looked away.

"I never told you this, but... I didn't stop you from confessing to Nutan because I hated you," she admitted.

I frowned, caught off guard. "Then why?"

Sheetal hesitated for a moment before answering.

"Because I was protecting her."

Her words sent a chill down my spine.

Protecting her?

From what? From me?

I didn't understand.

Sheetal must have seen the confusion in my eyes because she leaned forward, lowering her voice.

"There were things about Nutan that you didn't know, Sunil."

I gripped the edge of the table. "Then tell me. Tell me what I didn't know."

She looked down at her hands, her shoulders tensing, as if the truth was something heavy that she had been carrying for too long.

And then, finally, she spoke.

"When we left camp that day, Nutan was already engaged."

The words crashed over me like a tidal wave.

Engaged?

I blinked, shaking my head as if I had misheard her.

"That's... that's not possible."

But even as I said the words, I felt something crack inside me.

Sheetal gave me a sad smile. "It's the truth."

My throat went dry. "To who?"

"To a boy from her hometown Mapusa. Their families arranged it before she even joined the summer camp. She didn't tell anyone, not even me, until the last day."

I felt like the world had been ripped from under my feet.

All this time...

All these years...

I had been searching for someone who had already belonged to someone else.

The café suddenly felt too small. The air felt too thin. I wanted to stand up. I wanted to run, to escape this moment. But I couldn't move.

Instead, I let the words sink into my bones, let the reality settle in places I had never let it touch before. I had spent four years chasing a memory. Four years hoping that maybe, just maybe, she had been looking for me too. But she hadn't been.

She couldn't.

Because she had never been mine to begin with. Sheetal watched me carefully, as if waiting for me to break.

"I didn't tell you back then because... I didn't want to hurt you," she said gently. "And I didn't tell you now because I didn't know if you were ready to hear it."

I let out a short, hollow laugh. "And what made you think I was ready now?"

She sighed. "Because you deserved the truth."

I closed my eyes for a long moment, inhaling deeply, trying to breathe past the pain. When I opened them again, Sheetal was still there. She didn't say anything else. She just let me sit in the silence. And for the first time in four years, I felt something different. Not longing. Not hope. Not desperation. Just... acceptance.

I didn't cry. I didn't beg for answers. I didn't ask if Nutan had ever thought about me. Because in that moment, I realized it didn't matter anymore. Nutan was a part of my past. A beautiful part. A part that had shaped me, broken me, and rebuilt me in ways I had never understood before. But she wasn't my future. I had been chasing a ghost, holding onto a dream that had never been mine to keep.

And now?

Now, it was time to let her go. For the first time since that summer, I took a deep breath and exhaled. I looked at Sheetal, really looked at her. She had been there all along. A part of my past. A witness to my heartbreak. A reminder of where I had come from. And maybe, just maybe, a part of what was next. I gave her a small, tired smile.

"Thank you," I said softly.

She smiled back. "For what?"

"For telling me the truth," I said.

And with that, I finally let go.

As we stepped out of Raghuleela Mall, I felt lighter, not because the pain had disappeared, but because I finally understood. Some love stories aren't meant to last forever. Some are just meant to change you.

The evening sky had begun to darken, the city slowly transitioning into its neon-lit rhythm. The streets were alive, filled with the hum of conversations, the sound of rickshaws weaving through traffic, and the distant laughter of strangers.

Sheetal and I walked towards my Pulsar 150, the same bike I had borrowed from Ashutosh Kulkarni, not because I needed it, but because I wanted to impress her. There was something about tonight that felt different. As if we had stepped into another phase of our lives, leaving behind the ghosts of the past.

She hesitated for a moment before climbing onto the bike behind me. Her movements were careful, almost reluctant, as if she was afraid of something. And then, just as I started the engine, she did something unexpected.

She placed her hand on my shoulder.

It was a small gesture, barely noticeable, but I felt it like a spark igniting inside me. The warmth of her touch, the gentle pressure of her fingers, the unspoken trust behind it, it meant something. For a moment, I almost forgot to breathe.

She adjusted herself slightly, shifting closer, still uncomfortable, still cautious.

As I revved the engine, I deliberately pressed the brake harder than necessary when we hit the first speed breaker. I could feel her grip tighten, the sudden jolt making her hold onto me a little more firmly.

I didn't say a word.

But in that small moment, something shifted. Something fragile, something delicate. Maybe it was the way she trusted me in that instant. Maybe it was the way she didn't pull away. Maybe it was the way I suddenly didn't feel so alone anymore.

Instead of heading straight home, I turned the bike towards Sagar Vihar. Vashi had always been a city within a city, quieter than the rest of Mumbai, but still filled with life. And Sagar Vihar, that place was special.

It wasn't a grand beach like Juhu or Marine Drive, but it had its own magic. It was where the sea met the city in its quietest moments, where the air smelled of salt and wet earth, where the world slowed down just enough to make you feel like you had stepped outside of time.

We parked the bike near the entrance, walking towards the open stretch of land that overlooked the water. The sky had turned a deep shade of blue, the last remnants of daylight fading into the horizon. The waves lapped gently against the shore, their rhythm steady, comforting.

We didn't talk.

We didn't need to.

The silence between us wasn't uncomfortable. It was heavy with meaning.

I stopped by a small stall, buying a packet of chips. The vendor handed it to me with a knowing smile, as if he had seen a thousand people come here with their unspoken emotions, their unresolved pasts, their hearts full of things they couldn't say out loud.

We walked slowly, the gravel crunching under our feet, the wind playing with our hair.

She took a chip from the packet, eating it absentmindedly as she gazed at the sea.

There was something poetic about it, how two people, once tangled in the same past, now stood side by side, staring at the endless horizon of what could have been, what was, and what might be.

The air was cool, carrying with it the scent of rain that had fallen earlier in the evening. The lampposts lining the walkway flickered gently, casting long shadows on the ground.

We walked.

Sometimes close, sometimes with space between us.

Sometimes with our hands almost touching.

Sometimes not.

But the silence wasn't empty.

It was filled with the weight of years, with the memories of everything that had brought us to this moment. She picked up a small stone and skipped it across the water. It bounced twice before sinking beneath the surface. I did the same. The stone didn't bounce. It just sank. She smiled, the kind of smile that wasn't happy or sad, just understanding. We walked for two hours, moving between the past and the present, between old pain and new beginnings.

She told me about her life after camp.

I told her about mine.

We shared stories, not as the people we used to be, but as the people we had become.

It was late when I finally decided to drop her back. The city had quieted down, the roads emptier, the world softer under the glow of the streetlights. I rode carefully, neither of us speaking. Not because there was nothing to say, but because sometimes, silence says more than words ever can. As we neared her hostel, I slowed the bike to a stop just a few meters away from the entrance.

She didn't move to get off immediately.

I didn't rush her.

Something about this night felt unfinished, as if the universe was telling us not to say goodbye just yet.

She hesitated, her fingers brushing against my shoulder, as if she wanted to say something but couldn't find the words.

I could feel the warmth of her presence, the way the space between us was both too much and too little at the same time.

The night air was cool, carrying the scent of wet earth, the distant sound of a car passing by the quiet hum of a city that never truly slept.

Neither of us wanted to leave.

Neither of us wanted to end this moment.

But time, as always, was cruel.

Finally, she let out a small sigh, her fingers slipping away from my shoulder as she climbed off the bike.

She turned to face me, her eyes searching mine for something unspoken.

Maybe an answer.

Maybe a promise.

Maybe something she didn't even know she was looking for.

I wanted to say something, anything.

To tell her that tonight had meant something.

That it wasn't just a meeting, it wasn't just nostalgia, it wasn't just a night.

It was the beginning of something new.

But I didn't.

Because sometimes, the most beautiful things are the ones left unsaid.

She gave me a small smile, her eyes filled with something I couldn't quite place. And then, she turned and walked away. I watched her disappear behind the hostel gates, waiting until she was completely out of sight before finally exhaling. The engine roared as I pulled away, the road stretching ahead of me.

I didn't know where this was leading.

I didn't know what was happening between us.

But I knew one thing.

Tonight was the first time in years that I had felt something real.

Something that wasn't a memory. And for now... That was enough.

THIRTEEN

The First Signs of Something More

The night after I dropped Sheetal back at her hostel, I found myself unable to sleep. I lay in bed staring at the ceiling, the slow whir of the fan above me doing nothing to quiet the storm inside my chest. Something had changed. It wasn't just the way the night had unfolded; it was the way she made me feel. For the first time in years, my heart wasn't haunted by Nutan's absence.

For the first time in years, I wasn't stuck in the past. Instead, my mind was filled with Sheetal, her laughter, the way she tucked her hair behind her ear, the way she looked at me when she thought I wasn't noticing. There was something about her, something that felt dangerously familiar yet entirely new.

And that scared me. Because I had spent so long believing that my heart only belonged to Nutan. That my love story had ended before it even began. But now...

Now, I wasn't so sure anymore.

The next few days passed in a blur of routine. Classes. College assignments. Late-night rides. But something was different now. Every day, I found myself waiting for a message from Sheetal. Every evening, I hoped she would call. And when she didn't, I would scroll through my phone, debating whether or not I should text her first. I never did.

But fate had a way of intervening.

One evening, as I was sipping tea outside my hostel, my phone vibrated in my pocket. It was her.

Sheetal: "Are you free?"

Two simple words.

And yet, my heartbeat doubled.

I took a deep breath before replying.

Me: "Yeah. What's up?"

Sheetal: "Come to Bandstand. Near Mannat"

Bandstand.

I knew what that meant. "Mannat" Every Mumbaikar, every Bollywood fan, every dreamer knew Mannat. It wasn't just a house. It was a symbol. Shah Rukh Khan's home. The place where thousands gathered every single day, hoping to catch a glimpse of their hero. The place where dreams and reality blurred, where people stood with folded hands, treating it like a shrine. There were stories of fans waiting outside for hours, of people writing letters, of travelers coming from different parts of India just to stand outside those black gates and whisper a silent wish.

It was magical. And it was exactly the kind of place where Sheetal would ask me to meet her.

When I reached Bandstand, she was already there. Standing right in front of Mannat, staring at the nameplate as if it held the answers to all of life's questions. For a moment, I just watched her. The way the evening breeze played with her hair. The way her eyes reflected the soft glow of the streetlights. She didn't notice me at first, lost in her own world. And maybe, just maybe, I was losing myself in her. I took a step forward.

She turned.

And then, she smiled.

That was it.

That was all it took for my heart to betray me completely.

The crowd around Mannat was restless. Tourists and die-hard fans stood in groups, clicking pictures, whispering excitedly among themselves, waiting for a glimpse of their hero. The black iron gates stood tall, polished and grand, a silent guardian of the house behind them. Mannat was not just a home, it was a legend. A dream. A symbol of everything that Mumbai promised. It was a reminder that the city had the power to turn ordinary men into kings.

For a moment, I stood still, watching the people around me. Their eyes were filled with hope, their smiles wide with admiration. Some carried posters, some had written letters, and some just stood there, looking up at the house as if expecting Shah Rukh Khan himself to appear on the balcony and wave. The energy was infectious, yet somehow, I felt distant from it all. Sheetal stood beside me, looking up at the nameplate with quiet reverence. But her expression was different. She wasn't here for the same reason as the others.

She was lost in thought. After a few minutes, she turned and started walking towards the sea. And without a word, I followed.

Bandstand stretched before us, the Arabian Sea whispering softly against the rocks. The breeze carried the scent of salt and sand, wrapping around us like a familiar embrace. The water shimmered under the city lights, endless and deep, stretching towards the unknown. Neither of us spoke at first.

We just walked.

Side by side.

Step by step.

The city behind us, the sea ahead.

A song played faintly from someone's speaker in the distance. A slow melody, lost in the rhythm of the waves. The sound of crashing water mixed with the hum of Mumbai's night, car horns, distant laughter, the occasional train rumbling in the background. I stole a glance at her.

She looked... peaceful.

For the first time, since we reconnected, I saw a different side of Sheetal. The one that wasn't playful, teasing, or bold. The one that wasn't hiding behind her confident smiles.

She looked vulnerable.

And then, she spoke.

"I come here when I need to remind myself of home."

Her voice was soft, almost carried away by the wind. But I heard it.

And suddenly, everything made sense.

I looked at her, waiting for her to continue.

"I come here when I miss Goa," she admitted, her eyes locked on the horizon.

My heart skipped a beat. She was a Goan, just like me.

"I miss my parents," she continued. "I miss the way the sea in Goa smells after the rain. I miss the coconut trees, the quiet roads, the little cafés by the beach where time feels slower."

I understood exactly what she meant. Because I had felt it too. Mumbai was loud, restless, never stopping, never allowing you to breathe. It swallowed you whole, demanding all of you, forcing you to keep moving, to keep running.

But Goa... Goa was soft. It was home.

It was where mornings smelled of fresh bread and brewing chai, where the sea was not just a view but a friend. It was where sunsets felt like memories, not just the end of a day. I watched her as she wrapped her arms around herself, staring at the waves like they could take her back.

"This city is loud," she said again, her voice barely above a whisper. "It never stops. It never lets you breathe. But when I'm here, standing by the sea, I don't feel so lost."

A lump formed in my throat.

Because for the first time since coming to Mumbai, I realized, Maybe I wasn't the only one searching for something. Maybe she was searching too. Searching for home. Searching for something familiar. Searching for... herself.

Today, night air carried a rare coolness as we rode through its ever-awake streets. The roads, usually chaotic and unforgiving, felt quieter now, as if the city itself had slowed down just for us. Streetlights flickered in patterns along the route, their golden glow reflecting off the wet asphalt, remnants of the high tide licking the coastal roads.

She sat behind me, her presence soft yet tangible, her hands resting lightly on my shoulders. It was a simple touch, but I felt its weight. With every turn, every sudden jerk of the bike, every unexpected speed breaker, she tightened her grip, just slightly, just enough for me to notice. And I noticed everything. The way she shifted closer whenever the wind turned fierce, as if seeking warmth from something unspoken.

The way her breath tickled the nape of my neck when she sighed, lost in thoughts I wasn't privy to. The way she allowed herself to lean into me whenever we swerved, just for a second, just long enough to blur the lines between what was real and what was imagined. Mumbai stretched ahead, a never-ending symphony of honking rickshaws, distant train whistles, and the hum of neon signs that glowed against the darkness. The roads weren't empty, yet at this moment, it felt like it was just us.

A part of me wanted to break the silence. To say something, Something meaningful. Something that would make this night last forever. But words felt inadequate. Too small, too fragile.

So, I let the silence speak. And somehow, she understood.

The bike roared softly under us as we crossed the dimly lit roads of Bandra, past the sleeping chawls and the opulent mansions that stood in stark contrast to them. Mumbai was like that, a city of contradictions. The sea had been a witness to our unspoken emotions. The waves had carried our longing. Now, the city watched as we rode through its veins, wrapped in a stillness that only nights like these could bring. I could see the blurred outlines of Bandstand as we passed it again. The place where we had stood just moments ago. The place where she had revealed something raw, something real.

Her love for the sea.

Her longing for home.

Her confession, disguised as casual words, that this city didn't feel like hers.

And yet, here we were. Two people from the same roots, trying to belong to a place that wasn't ours. Two strangers who were slowly becoming something more.

As I turned into the quiet lane where her hostel stood, I slowed the bike to a gentle stop. The street was empty except for a lone streetlamp, its dull yellow glow casting long shadows. The hostel gates stood in front of us, tall and silent, as if waiting for this moment to play out. She stepped down from the bike, hesitating. For a moment, neither of us spoke.

Neither of us wanted to break the spell that the night had cast over us. She adjusted her bag on her shoulder, brushing a few strands of hair away from her face, looking at me as if waiting for something.

A word.

A sign.

Something to acknowledge that this night had changed things.

But I remained silent.

Because what could I say?

That I had felt something shift between us?

That I had noticed every single moment?

That I had memorized the way she held me just a little tighter than she needed to?

Instead, I just watched as she lingered near the gate.

Then, just before she turned to walk away, she turned back.

And in that one second, everything changed.

Because in her eyes, I saw it.

The same hesitation.

The same longing.

The same confusion that mirrored my own.

It was terrifying. It was thrilling.

It was something neither of us were ready to name yet.

But it was there.

Unspoken.

Lingering.

Real.

Maybe, just maybe,

This wasn't just friendship anymore.

This was something else.

Something we weren't ready to name yet.

FOURTEEN

When Friendship Crosses the Line

Oct – 2008,

Mumbai was changing. Or maybe, I was changing. The city no longer felt like the chaotic beast I had struggled to tame when I first arrived. The trains still ran late, the crowds still pushed and shoved, and the streets still never slept. But amidst all of this, I had found a rhythm, a rhythm that revolved around her. And now, I had something new to match this new life. I finally bought my first bike.

No more borrowing from Ashutosh, no more waiting for someone else's schedule to align with mine.

It was mine. A Pulsar 220 CC, The dream bike of every young man back then. If you had a Pulsar 220CC, you weren't just another guy on the road, you were someone. It was the fastest Indian bike at that time, and riding it felt like I had conquered something. The first time I sat on it, gripping the handles, feeling the smooth power beneath me, I knew, this wasn't just a bike.

It was freedom.

The deep growl of the engine, the smooth acceleration, the way it cut through Mumbai's madness like a knife through butter, it was intoxicating. And the best part?

She loved it too.

Days passed, and my life had settled into something dangerously comfortable. Every evening, after her shift at Hotel Taj Colaba, I would ride through the city, past honking rickshaws, and tired officegoers, until I reached Bandra. By the time I pulled up near her hostel, she would already be waiting outside. She always spotted me before I saw her. The second our eyes met, she would smile, a small, knowing smile that sent a rush of warmth through me. And just like that, we became inseparable.

This city had thousands of cafés, but we kept returning to the same one, a small, hidden gem in Carter Road that had a perfect view of the sea. It was never crowded, just a few artists sketching, some writers lost in their own worlds, and couples whispering over cups of coffee. It became our place. She would always order cold coffee, and I would tease her, "Only kids drink cold coffee," while sipping my steaming hot chai.

She would roll her eyes, laughing. "At least I'm not burning my tongue every day like you."

It was harmless. Playful. Familiar. But familiarity is dangerous. Because soon, we weren't just two friends having coffee.

Soon, I started noticing the way she absentmindedly played with her hair when she was thinking. The way she bit her lip when she was nervous. The way she leaned a little closer when she was telling me a story, her voice dropping to a whisper as if we were sharing a secret. And I knew, I knew something had changed.

Because for the first time, I wasn't just looking at Sheetal, my friend.

I was looking at Sheetal, the girl who had slowly become my favourite part of the day.

This city was different at that night. The crowds thinned, the roads opened, and the air was softer, carrying the scent of the sea instead of gasoline fumes. After our café visits, we started riding through the city, nowhere in particular, just riding. With her behind me on the bike, her hands resting lightly on my shoulders, her voice mixing with the hum of the engine, I felt something I hadn't felt in a long time.

Peace.

We drove past Marine Drive, the Queen's Necklace stretching endlessly before us, the water shimmering in the moonlight. Past Juhu Beach, where the smell of freshly roasted bhutta filled the air, and street musicians played Bollywood songs for lovers walking hand in hand. And sometimes, when the night was too perfect, we stopped at Worli Sea Face, sitting by the promenade, watching the city sleep. She would hug her knees, resting her chin on them, looking at the horizon. And I would steal glances at her when she wasn't looking. Because I knew, this wasn't just friendship anymore.

That night, air was thick with the scent of rain. The streets shimmered under the soft glow of streetlights, the mist of drizzle turning the city into a dreamscape of blurred neon and glistening asphalt. Mumbai, a city that never slept, seemed to hold its breath in the aftermath of a fresh rain, as if savoring the silence that was so rare within its boundaries. I rode through the quiet lanes, feeling the cool air graze my face, the rhythmic hum of the engine beneath me blending with the distant sounds of the Arabian Sea. She sat behind me, closer than usual, her fingers barely gripping the sides of my jacket. It wasn't a tight hold, not something desperate or hesitant, just a gentle, casual presence, enough to make my heart beat a little faster.

Then, out of nowhere, her voice broke through the quiet hum of the night.

"Let's not go back yet," she said softly.

I slowed the bike, stealing a glance at her reflection in the mirror. Her face was calm, but her eyes held something different tonight, something restless, something longing.

"Where do you want to go?" I asked, my voice steady despite the storm raging inside me.

She smiled, that mischievous, almost childlike smile she had whenever she was about to do something impulsive. "Anywhere," she said. "Just not home."

I didn't question her. I didn't ask why. Because truth be told, I didn't want the night to end either. So, without another word, I turned the bike and headed toward Sagar Vihar.

The rain had slowed to a light drizzle, soft and delicate, like a whisper against the skin. Aksa beach, usually buzzing with evening walkers and young couples stealing moments of quiet romance, was almost deserted. The waves lapped against the rocks gently, the moonlight reflecting in broken silver shards over the water.

We parked the bike and walked along the promenade, the air heavy with the scent of wet earth and salt. The streetlights flickered through the mist, casting long, ghostly shadows.

She walked beside me, her steps light, almost playful. There was something about the way she carried herself tonight, something weightless, as if she had let go of something she had been holding onto for too long.

We stopped at a small roadside stall and bought a packet of chips. She tore it open carelessly, offering me some without a word. We ate as we walked, the sound of waves filling the spaces between our conversations.

And we talked. About childhood memories, the monsoon days in Goa, where the sea roared louder, and the streets smelled of damp earth and fresh pakoras. About dreams, how she had once wanted to be a pilot but settled for hospitality instead. About losses, the people who had come and gone from our lives, the ones who had left behind empty spaces that no one else could fill.

And at some point, as if it was the most natural thing in the world, she slipped her arm through mine. It wasn't dramatic, not an intentional move meant to make a statement. It was casual, instinctive, as if she had done it a hundred times before. I felt my breath catch. The warmth of her skin against mine, the way her fingers curled so lightly around my arm, it was maddening in the softest, sweetest way possible.

I didn't move away.

I didn't even breathe.

Because in that moment, I felt it.

This was more than just friendship now.

The boundary we had both carefully tiptoed around was slowly, silently vanishing into the mist around us.

But neither of us was ready to say it.

Not yet.

Two hours passed in what felt like minutes.

When I finally convinced her it was late, we walked back to the bike, our footsteps slower than before. The air had turned cooler, the rain now just a memory lingering in the dampness of the night.

She sat behind me as I started the bike, and this time, she held onto me differently. It wasn't just a light touch anymore. Her arms wrapped around me, not too tight, not too loose, just enough to make my pulse quicken. The city was asleep, the roads almost empty. I could hear her breathing behind me, steady and soft, her warmth pressing into my back. I rode slower than usual. Not because I was afraid of the wet roads. But because I didn't want this ride to end.

Every turn, every speed breaker, she adjusted herself, leaning into me slightly, her fingers pressing lightly against my chest. The touch was delicate, unintentional yet deliberate, an echo of something we both felt but didn't dare name. Mumbai blurred past us in golden streetlights and neon signs, but all I could feel was her. And in the stillness of that ride, I realized something terrifyingly beautiful, She wasn't just someone I had reconnected with, She wasn't just a friend from the past, She was becoming something more, Something I wasn't sure I was ready for.

Something that was starting to consume me.

When we reached her hostel, I stopped the bike, expecting her to step down immediately. But she didn't, She sat there, silent, I felt her hesitate behind me, her fingers still resting against my jacket. Then, slowly, she exhaled, pulling off her helmet. And instead of stepping down, she turned to face me, The streetlight above us cast a warm glow over her face, highlighting the damp strands of hair clinging to her forehead, the softness in her expression, And for the first time, I noticed how her eyes looked at night.

Darker. Deeper.

Like an ocean I could get lost in, I wanted to say something, Maybe joke about how she should finally admit I was her favorite person in Mumbai. Maybe tell her that this, whatever this was, was no longer something I could ignore, Maybe just say her name. But before I could, she smiled. a soft, almost shy smile, And in that moment, I knew.

I wasn't the only one feeling this shift between us. I wasn't the only one scared of how easily she had slipped into my life, This wasn't just friendship anymore. This was something else.

Something neither of us was ready to name.

Something dangerous.

Something beautiful.

She finally stepped down, adjusting her bag over her shoulder, still not looking away. She turned toward the hostel gates, taking slow steps, as if she was waiting for me to stop her.

I didn't.

And just before she disappeared inside, she turned back, one last glance, One last moment that changed everything.

Because in her eyes, I saw it. The same question, The same confusion, The same silent, terrifying, wonderful possibility.

And as I rode away, the night air cool against my face, I realized something. Whatever was happening between us, whatever we were too afraid to admit, Whatever line we had just crossed.

The rain had started to fall again, heavier this time, soaking the pavement, turning the night into a shimmering blur of silver and gold. I sat there on my bike, motionless, watching her disappear through the hostel gates. I should have left. I should have started the engine, driven away, let the night swallow whatever had just happened between us.

But I didn't.

I stayed.

I don't know why. Maybe because something about that last glance haunted me. Maybe because my heart refused to accept that this was how the night would end.

So, I waited.

The raindrops drummed against my shoulders, soaking through my shirt, slipping down my skin in cold, unrelenting streams. The street was empty, the only sound was the distant hum of traffic and the occasional roll of thunder above.

And then,

I heard footsteps.

Soft, hurried, hesitant.

I turned.

And there she was.

Running back towards me, the rain clinging to her like a second skin, her hair dripping, her breath uneven, she stopped just inches away, looking at me like she had made a decision she didn't fully understand yet. Then, before I could say a word, she hugged me, Not the kind of hug friends share, not something casual, or light, or fleeting, this was different, this was everything.

Her arms wrapped around me tightly, her fingers pressing into my back, as if she was afraid that if she let go, I would disappear. And I held her too, without thinking, without questioning, because in that moment, there was nothing else, No past, No future, No unspoken fears.

Just her. Just us...

The rain poured around us, drenching us both, but neither of us moved. The city could have burned down around us, and I wouldn't have noticed. Her body was warm against mine, her heartbeat erratic, matching the storm raging inside me. And then, it happened, she pulled back slightly, just enough to look up at me, And in the next second, her lips found mine, A hesitant touch.

Soft. Trembling.

Like she wasn't sure if this was real.

Like she wasn't sure if this was a mistake.

But I kissed her back.

Gently. Slowly.

As if time had stopped.

As if this was inevitable.

As if every moment, every glance, every silence between us had led to this.

The rain blurred everything, the world, the night, the logic that told me this shouldn't be happening.

But I didn't care.

Because nothing had ever felt more right.

She pulled away first, just a little, her breath warm against my lips.

She didn't speak.

She didn't need to.

The way she looked at me said everything.

This wasn't just a mistake.

This wasn't just the rain, or the night, or the loneliness of a city that never stopped moving.

This was real.

Something had changed between us forever.

And there was no going back now.

FIFTEEN

The Night That Changed Everything

The rain hadn't stopped. It kept falling around us, washing away the night's silence, drowning the words we couldn't say. She stood there, her breath uneven, her lips still trembling from the kiss we had just shared. The hostel gate was behind her, safety and familiarity just a few steps away. But she didn't move.

Neither did I. The world felt different now.

Something had shifted, something fragile, something dangerous, something beautiful.

I could still feel the warmth of her lips, the softness of her touch, the way she had held onto me like she was afraid to let go. And I was afraid to move, afraid that if I did, this moment would slip away like a dream, dissolving into the rain and vanishing into the night.

She swallowed hard, her hands still lightly gripping my jacket, as if anchoring herself to this reality.

Her eyes searched mine, looking for something, reassurance, understanding, or maybe just a reason to believe that what had just happened wasn't a mistake.

But I didn't know what to say.

What could I say?

That I had wanted to kiss her from the moment we had reconnected? That I had felt something shift inside me every time she looked at me? That, despite everything, despite Nutan, despite the past, this felt more real than anything else had in years?

No.

I couldn't say any of that, Because I didn't even understand it myself. So, instead, I just stood there, watching her, waiting for her to decide what happened next.

And then,

She let go.

She took a small step back, her fingers slipping away from my jacket, her gaze flickering down to the wet pavement between us.

"I..." she started but then stopped.

I held my breath, waiting.

She looked up again, and there was something in her eyes, fear, maybe, or hesitation. But also... something else.

Something unspoken, something that made my pulse race. She took another step back, towards the hostel gate.

Then another.

I knew she was about to leave. And I should have let her, I should have smiled, said goodnight, let her walk away.

But I didn't.

Instead, I reached for her hand.

I don't know why.

I just... did.

And for a second, just one second, she let me.

Our fingers barely touched, a whisper of warmth in the cold night air.

And then,

She pulled away.

She turned, walked to the gate, and without looking back,

She disappeared inside.

I didn't leave right away, I sat on my bike for a long time, staring at the gate, hoping she would come back out, Hoping she would say something, Hoping she would give me a reason to believe that tonight had meant as much to her as it had to me, But she didn't.

The rain fell harder, soaking through my clothes, making my skin cold, But the fire inside me refused to die, Something had happened tonight, Something neither of us had planned for, Something that felt like the beginning of something new.

Or maybe... the beginning of the end.

I didn't know which yet.

And that terrified me.

Mumbai didn't stop for love; it didn't pause for heartbreak. It didn't care about the restless night I had spent, tossing and turning, thinking about her, the city moved forward, always forward, And I had no choice but to move with it.

But my mind was elsewhere, all morning, as I went through my routine, college, lectures, assignments, I kept waiting for my phone to buzz, for a message, for something, but it never did, she didn't text, she didn't call, she didn't even leave a scrap on Orkut.

And that silence...

That silence killed me.

It was almost evening when my phone finally buzzed, I grabbed it immediately, my heart racing, It was her.

Sheetal: Can we meet?

I stared at the message, my mind spinning.

After the way last night had ended, I didn't know what to expect.

Did she regret it?

Did she want to pretend it never happened?

Or...

Did she want more?

I typed back quickly.

Me: Where?

Her reply came almost instantly.

Sheetal: Same place. Bandstand.

When I reached Bandstand, she was already there., Standing near the sea, arms wrapped around herself, staring out at the waves, for a second, I just watched her, she looked different today, not in her clothes, not in her posture, in her eyes, there was something there, something heavy, something she was struggling to say.

I walked up to her, my footsteps quiet against the wet pavement.

She didn't turn, didn't say anything, So, I stood beside her, waiting, Letting the sea speak for us.

Then, finally, She exhaled.

"I didn't sleep last night," she admitted softly.

Neither did I.

But I didn't say that she turned to face me then, her eyes searching mine, "What are we doing, Sunil?" she asked.

I swallowed hard, because I didn't have an answer, but I knew one thing, I didn't want to lose her.

Not now, not after everything.

So, instead of answering, instead of speaking, instead of thinking, I reached for her hand again.

And this time, she didn't pull away.

The next day, Sheetal called me again, this time with a request. "Sunil, my parents are coming to town tomorrow. Can you pick her up from the station?"

"Of course," I agreed without hesitation. The following afternoon, I made my way to the station, anticipation mingling with a bit of nervousness. Meeting Sheetal's family felt like a significant step in our friendship. When her mom arrived, I recognized her instantly from the descriptions Sheetal had given me. She was a warm, kind woman, her eyes twinkling with the same spark of life that I saw in Sheetal. We exchanged greetings and I drove her to their place. Her dad, a stern yet kind-hearted man, and her younger brother, who seemed to have inherited Sheetal's mischievous grin. They welcomed me like an old friend, and we spent the evening sharing stories and laughter. It felt like I was part of their family.

As Sheetal's internship start date approached, our meetings became more frequent. We spent hours discussing her future at the Taj, the experiences she would gain, and the people she would meet. Each conversation was filled with excitement and a touch of apprehension.

The day before her internship began, Sheetal and I took a walk along Marine Drive. The setting sun bathed the Arabian Sea in a golden glow, mirroring the warmth in our hearts. We talked about everything, our dreams, our fears, and our hopes for the future.

"I'm going to miss our regular hangouts," I admitted as we strolled along the promenade.

"Me too," she replied softly. "But this is just the beginning, Sunil. We'll still meet. And I promise to keep you updated about everything."

The next morning, I drove her to the Taj on my Pulsar. As we approached the grand entrance, I could see the awe in her eyes. This was it, the start of a new chapter in her life. We exchanged a quick hug before she stepped off the bike, her face a mix of excitement and determination. Watching her walk into the hotel, I felt a swell of pride and a touch of melancholy. Our friendship had grown so much, and now she was embarking on a new journey. But I knew this was just a part of our friendship. We had shared so many moments, and there were many more to come.

In the following weeks, we kept in touch regularly. She shared her experiences at the Taj, the new skills she was learning, and the interesting people she was meeting. Each story she told me made me feel like I was right there with her, cheering her on. Through it all, one thing remained constant, my hope that one day, through her, I might find Nutan. But for now, I was content to support Sheetal and cherish the bond we had forged, a bond that was growing stronger with each passing day.

My regular routine was to pick her up from the Hotel Taj, and today her shift ended around 9 o'clock. As I rode my Pulsar, I was dressed in a casual yet stylish ensemble: a well-fitted t-shirt that clung to my frame, blue jeans that had seen many adventures, and a pair of worn yet comfortable sports shoes. Despite the late hour, I wore my sunglasses, adding a touch of mystery and a stud-like appearance to my look.

The weather that night was on the cusp of change. The air was thick with anticipation, the kind that makes your skin tingle. Clouds hung low in the sky, heavy and dark, signalling that a downpour was imminent. A gentle breeze carried the scent of rain, mingling with the faint aroma of wet earth. It was one of those nights where you could feel nature holding its breath, waiting for the heavens to open. She emerged from the staff entry and exit gate of the hotel, her eyes lighting up as she spotted me. I smiled, a gesture that she returned with a warmth that made my heart race. She climbed onto my Pulsar, settling behind me with a familiarity that had become our routine.

As we rode through the streets of Mumbai, she reached into her bag and pulled out her iPod. She handed me one side of her headphones, keeping the other for herself, and then selected a song. The opening notes of "Akhiyon Ke Jharokhon Se" filled our ears, creating a cocoon of music around us. The melody was hauntingly beautiful, and it felt like the perfect soundtrack to our ride.

The sky rumbled, a low growl of thunder in the distance, and within moments, the first drops of rain began to fall. I pulled over to a spot with a small overhang, providing us with just enough shelter to escape the downpour. The rain came down in sheets, the sound of it hitting the ground creating a rhythm that matched the beating of my heart. We stood there, huddled together under the makeshift shelter, the rain creating a curtain around us. The world outside seemed to fade away, leaving just the two of us in our little bubble. The music continued to play, its soft strains mixing with the sound of the rain, creating a symphony that was both melancholic and hopeful.

I turned to look at her, her face illuminated by the glow of the iPad. Her eyes sparkled with the same excitement and joy that I felt. We didn't need words; the silence between us was filled with understanding and connection. The rain, the music, the shared headphone. it was a moment of pure, unspoken intimacy. We listened to the song in its entirety, lost in the magic of the moment. As the rain began to ease, I looked at her and smiled, a smile that she returned with a warmth that melted my heart. I knew then, in that fleeting moment, that this was a memory I would cherish forever.

As the rain slowed to a gentle drizzle, we got back on my bike and continued our ride, the night air cool and fresh. The streets glistened with the remnants of the rain, and the city seemed to have been washed clean. We didn't need to speak; the shared experience had deepened our bond in a way that words never could. That night, as I dropped her off at her flat, I felt a sense of contentment that I hadn't known before. Our friendship had grown into something beautiful, and I knew that, whatever the future held, this moment would remain etched in my heart forever. The rain, the music, and the shared headphone had woven a memory that was as romantic as any poetry, a testament to the magic of unspoken love and connection.

That night, when I dropped her off at her home, it again started raining. She asked me to come up to her flat on the third floor, but I declined, saying I'd wait outside for 5-10 minutes to smoke a sutta before heading home. She decided to wait with me. The rain intensified, and the cold air made us both shiver. The weather was chilling, with flashes of lightning illuminating the dark sky. Suddenly, a particularly loud crack of thunder startled her, and she immediately hugged me. Instinctively, I hugged her back. As she clung to me, she put her hand on my shoulder, her entire body nestled in my arms. It felt as if she had surrendered herself completely. Her lips were trembling, and her eyes were cast down. It was a deeply intimate moment, filled with the electricity of the storm and the warmth of our embrace. The rain poured around us, but in that moment, all I could feel was the closeness and the unspoken connection between us.

Then, in the midst of the rain and the cold, our eyes met. There was an unspoken understanding, a pull we couldn't resist. Slowly, as if drawn by an invisible force, our faces inched closer. Her breath mingled with mine, warm and sweet against the chill of the night. And then, without either of us intending it, our lips met. It was soft and tentative at first, a gentle brush that sent a thrill through my entire being. The rain continued to pour around us, but in that moment, we were lost in each other. The kiss deepened, becoming more passionate, as if we were trying to convey all the emotions that words could never express. Her hands moved to the back of my neck, pulling me closer, and I wrapped my arms around her, feeling the warmth of her body against mine. We stayed like that for what felt like an eternity, kissing in the rain, completely absorbed in each other. When we finally pulled away, we were both breathless, our foreheads resting together, eyes closed. The world around us seemed to fade away, leaving just the two of us in that perfect, unforgettable moment.

After that night, something changed inside me. As I rode back to my hostel, the rain still pouring down, my mind was a whirlwind of conflicting emotions. I couldn't shake the feeling that I had done something terribly wrong. My thoughts were consumed by guilt and confusion. How could I have kissed Sheetal when my heart belonged to Nutan? The kiss, which felt so right in the moment, now seemed like a betrayal. I kept replaying the scene in my head, the way her lips had felt against mine, the warmth of her embrace, but each memory was tainted by a growing sense of shame. I felt as though I had taken advantage of her, that I had crossed a line that shouldn't have been crossed.

What if she felt the same?

What if our friendship was ruined because of my actions?

As I reached my hostel, my roommate Ashutosh immediately noticed my distress.

"What happened, man? You look like you've seen a ghost," he said,

But I couldn't bring myself to explain.

The whole ride home, I had been haunted by the thought that I had hurt Sheetal, that she might never want to see me again. The idea of losing her friendship was unbearable.

The next few days were torturous. I waited for her call, but it never came. Each silent day that passed only amplified my fears.

Had I scared her away?

Did she regret the kiss as much as I did?

My mind was a battlefield of doubt and remorse. I felt as if I had shattered something beautiful and irreplaceable. The lack of communication between us was deafening. Every time my phone rang, my heart leapt with hope, only to be crushed when it wasn't her. I couldn't focus on anything else, my studies, my friends, nothing could distract me from the gnawing anxiety.

I was convinced that she must be feeling the same way, hurt and confused, and I blamed myself entirely. I was overwhelmed with the thought that I had lost a dear friend, that my impulsive actions had driven a wedge between us. I kept replaying the moment in my mind, wondering what I could have done differently. The memory of our kiss, which had once felt so magical, now felt like a curse.

As days turned into weeks, the silence remained. It felt as if a part of me was missing, as if I was floating in a sea of uncertainty. The bond we had shared, the laughter and the countless hours spent together, now seemed like a distant dream. The more I thought about it, the more I feared that I had irreparably damaged our relationship. I missed her presence, her laughter, and the comfort of our friendship. The guilt weighed heavily on me, and I couldn't shake the feeling that I had betrayed both her and Nutan.

In my heart, I knew I had to make things right, but I didn't know how. The fear of losing her for good was a constant ache, a reminder of my mistake. Every night, I lay awake, wishing I could turn back time, wishing I could take back that moment and preserve our friendship. But reality was relentless, and I had to face the consequences of my actions. I hoped, with all my heart, that she would understand and that we could find a way to move past this. Until then, I was trapped in my own mind, tormented by what might have been.

It was an evening of 26th November, Mumbai was bustling with its usual energy as I returned to my hostel room after a long day of college. Ashutosh and our friends were gathered, sharing stories and laughter, unaware of the impending tragedy that would soon unfold.Around 9:30 PM, Praveen's urgent knocks disrupted our peaceful evening. "Turn on the TV, quick!" he exclaimed.

Confused, we complied, and within moments, the screen was filled with scenes of horror and chaos. News channels blared with updates of terrorists rampaging through CST station, indiscriminately taking lives. The images were surreal and killing nnocent people caught in the crossfire, their lives cut short in an instant. As we watched in disbelief, the horror spread. The terrorists moved methodically, striking at the heart of Mumbai's landmarks, the iconic Taj and Oberoi Hotels. Flames licked the night sky, sirens wailed, and ambulances raced through the streets. The city was under siege, gripped by fear and uncertainty.

Amidst the chaos, my phone buzzed incessantly with calls from worried family and friends, their voices filled with panic. I tried calling Sheetal, hoping for her safety, but there was no answer. Fear tightened its grip on my heart as reports came in that the terrorists had breached Hotel Taj, where Sheetal had recently begun her internship.

The scenes on TV were devastating smoke billowing from shattered windows, survivors recounting tales of horror and heroism, emergency responders rushing to aid the injured. Each moment felt like an eternity as Mumbai's resilience was put to the test in the face of unimaginable tragedy. Streets once bustling with life now lay silent, except for the wail of sirens and the distant cries of anguish. Mumbai, a city known for its spirit and strength, was now a battlefield where innocent lives hung in the balance. Through the night, prayers mingled with tears as we awaited news of loved ones and hoped for an end to the bloodshed. The toll of lives lost continued to rise, each death a stark reminder of the fragility of life and the brutality of terrorism.

The ringing of my phone shattered the eerie silence that had settled over me. It was Sheetal's mother, her voice fraught with worry and fear.

"Sunil, where is Sheetal? Is she safe?" Her words echoed my own frantic thoughts, amplifying the helplessness of not knowing.

I tried desperately to reach Sheetal, each call met with agonizing silence on the other end. Her phone, usually quick to answer, now seemed deaf to my pleas. I dialed her roommate next, hoping for some solace, only to hear the same painful refrain: "She's in the hotel, but she's not answering."

Fear tightened its grip around my heart, each moment without news feeling like an eternity.

The television flickered in the background, a relentless stream of chaos and despair playing out across Mumbai. Images of smoke-filled corridors and shattered glass mirrored the turmoil within me. My mind raced with scenarios, Sheetal trapped, injured, or worse. Each possibility tearing at my resolve. I paced the room, my thoughts consumed by the worst-case scenarios. Tears welled up unbidden, silent prayers escaping my lips as I pleaded for her safety.

Mumbai, a city once vibrant and alive, now felt like a battleground where terror reigned unchecked. Hours blurred into an agonizing vigil, every passing minute etching deeper lines of worry on my face. The city outside remained a cacophony of sirens and distant gunfire, a stark contrast to the suffocating stillness within me. In that moment, all that mattered was Sheetal's safety, her absence a void I couldn't bear.

The relentless chaos of the terrorist attack enveloped Mumbai as the clock struck 1 AM. Anxiety gripped me tightly; Sheetal's whereabouts were unknown, and my heart pounded with worry. Determined to ensure her safety, I hastily mounted my bike, driven by a desperate need to find her. Ashutosh appeared beside me, his voice filled with concern, pleading for me to reconsider. Tears streamed down my face as I insisted, "I must go to Hotel Taj. Sheetal needs me. I can't sit here and wait." Ashutosh understood my resolve and joined me on the bike. Together, we embarked on a harrowing journey towards Hotel Taj. The streets, typically bustling, were eerily deserted, illuminated only by sporadic police lights. Approaching Mankhurd, and then nearing Chembur, our path was abruptly blocked by a barricade of officers. Their uniforms gleamed in the dim light as they sternly denied us entry, fearing for our safety amid the ongoing crisis. My pleas fell on deaf ears as they shouted warnings and demands to turn back. Desperation surged within me, my voice cracking with emotion as I implored them, "Sheetal is inside. I have to reach her. Please let us through!" The officers remained resolute, unmoved by my distress. Tears of helplessness mingled with the rain, each drop echoing my anguish. The city, usually vibrant and alive, now echoed with sirens and the distant echoes of gunfire. Every passing second felt like an eternity, my heart torn between fear for Sheetal's safety and frustration at being unable to reach her.

The night was thick with tension and fear as I stood by the police barricade, straining to hear any news. Every passing second felt like an eternity, my heart pounding with dread until finally, my phone buzzed with Sheetal's name.

"Sheetal?" I answered urgently, my voice cracking with emotion.

"Sunil," her voice trembled through the phone, barely audible over the chaos.

"Sheetal, where are you? Are you safe?" I asked, my voice betraying the fear gripping my soul.

There was a moment of silence, broken only by distant echoes of gunfire.

Then, in a trembling voice, she whispered, "Sunil, do you know... I love you. I love you so much.

My breath caught in my throat, tears welling in my eyes as I struggled to find my voice.

"Sheetal," I managed to choke out, my heart breaking with every syllable, "I love you too. More than anything."

The line crackled with static, our words hanging in the air between us, heavy with unspoken fears and unshed tears. And then, as suddenly as it had begun, the call dropped. I frantically tried calling her back, but there was no answer, only the hollow emptiness of a disconnected line.

The morning sun struggled to penetrate the lingering haze of smoke that blanketed Mumbai. I sat transfixed before the television, the scenes of destruction and chaos from the previous night playing out in a relentless loop. The city, known for its resilience, had been rattled to its core by the ruthless acts of terror. Amidst the grim updates and the haunting footage of the attack's aftermath, a solemn announcement resonated through the airwaves: "We mourn the loss of brave souls." The names reverberated like thunder in my ears, Hemant Karkare, Ashok Kamte, Vijay Salaskar, Tukaram Omble, Shashank Shinde. The heroes who had stood unwavering against the onslaught, their lives extinguished in the line of duty. Their images flashed across the screen, each frame a poignant reminder of their courage and sacrifice. They had charged into the heart of danger, confronting terror with unyielding resolve. The nation grieved their loss, yet their legacy blazed brightly, a beacon of valour and patriotism that refused to be extinguished by the darkness of violence.

But amidst this national tragedy, my heart bled with a more personal anguish. Sheetal's safety hung by a fragile thread amidst the chaos gripping the city. Her voice from our last phone call echoed hauntingly in my mind, her words trembling with fear and love: "Sunil, I love you so much..." In that fleeting moment, amidst the distant echoes of gunshots, our declarations of love were swallowed by the tumult. The call abruptly ended, leaving me grasping at the silence, desperately yearning for any sign that she remained unharmed.

It was the morning of 29th November, three agonizing days since terror had gripped Mumbai in its deadly embrace. The entire nation held its breath, mourning the heroes lost and praying for the safety of their loved ones. Amidst this collective anxiety, a ray of grim relief pierced through the darkness, news spread like wildfire that the terrorists had been neutralized, Mumbai was free once more. Yet, amidst the city's tentative sighs of relief, our hearts were heavy with a different kind of dread.

There had been no word from Sheetal since that harrowing phone call amidst gunfire. Her absence weighed on us like an unbearable burden, each passing moment etching deeper lines of worry on our faces. Sheetal's mother had arrived in Mumbai, her eyes haunted with fear and hope. The days dragged on in a haze of uncertainty, our nerves frayed by the waiting.

Then, finally, a phone call shattered the uneasy silence, and with trembling hands, Sheetal's mother answered. The voice on the other end delivered a blow that reverberated through our souls, Sheetal was no more. A wave of anguish swept over us as we struggled to comprehend the enormity of the loss. She had fought bravely, they said, saving the lives of three foreigners amidst the chaos. In the line of duty, two bullets had struck her down, a poignant testament to her courage and selflessness. As the news sank in, grief consumed us. Her mother's cries echoed through the corridors of the hospital where we gathered, their raw intensity a stark contrast to the sterile surroundings. Sheetal's father stood stoically beside her, his eyes betraying the pain that words could not express. Her brother, silent and devastated, clung to the last shreds of disbelief. And then, after three excruciating days, we were faced with the heart-wrenching task of bringing Sheetal home. We stood by, helpless witnesses to the finality of it all, as her lifeless body was gently lifted, a solemn procession through the city streets that had witnessed both her valour and her untimely end. In those moments, Mumbai's resilience felt fragile, our grief mingling with a fierce pride in Sheetal's bravery. She had not just been a victim of senseless violence; she had become a symbol of unwavering courage and sacrifice in the face of terror.

SIXTEEN

<u>**And Here I am...**</u>

As I stood by Sheetal's final resting place, surrounded by the weight of grief and the echo of her last words, "I love you," I found myself engulfed in a whirlwind of memories. Her voice, gentle yet determined, lingered in my mind like a bittersweet melody. Each moment we had shared flooded back, her laughter, her warmth, her unwavering spirit. Sheetal's departure had left an indelible mark on my soul. In her absence, I realized the depth of what we had shared, the love that had blossomed amidst life's tumultuous currents. Her final words echoed a truth that now resonated deeply within me, true love, once found, should be cherished and celebrated every single day.

As I stand here, grappling with the profound absence of both Sheetal and Nutan from my life, I reflect on the intricacies of love and the paths we choose. Sheetal's departure has left me with a poignant realization, a realization that evokes both sorrow and wisdom. When Sheetal was by my side, my heart often wandered elsewhere, oblivious to the depth of her love. From the days of our shared memories at summer camps to the present moment, she remained steadfast in her affection, while I failed to fully recognize the treasure I held in my hands. Now, as I navigate a world without either Sheetal or Nutan,

I am reminded of the fragility of time and the regret that comes with lost opportunities. Sheetal's love was a constant, a beacon of unwavering devotion that illuminated my path, even when I failed to acknowledge its brilliance.

As I stood by the quiet shores, the memories of Nutan and Sheetal echoed through my mind like the waves crashing gently against the rocks. In the silence of my solitude, I realized the profound lessons my journey had taught me.

Nutan, the girl whose laughter once filled my days with joy, remained a bittersweet memory. I never found the courage to tell her how I truly felt, and she drifted away like a passing dream, leaving behind a lingering sense of regret.

Then came Sheetal, whose love I only understood in the shadow of tragedy. Her final words, whispered amidst chaos and despair, echoed in my heart forever. "I love you, Sunil," she had said, her voice trembling with emotion. Yet, those words had come too late, drowned out by the harsh realities of life.

Now, standing alone with only memories as my companions, my message to the youth resonates with deep conviction. "Cherish the ones who love you," I would tell them. "Don't wait for tomorrow to express your feelings. Value every moment you have with those who care for you, for life is fleeting, and love is fragile."

I understand now that love isn't just a feeling; it's an action. It's about showing up, being present, and letting those we care about know how much they mean to us every day. I have learned this lesson through heartache and loss, but it's a lesson I wish to impart to others, so they wouldn't have to learn it the hard way. As the sun dipped below the horizon, casting a golden glow over the waters, I made a silent vow to honour the love I had known and lost. In doing so, I hope to inspire others to embrace their own journeys of love with courage, appreciation, and an unwavering commitment to living without regrets.

To the youth who may read this, I offer this heartfelt plea: cherish the love that graces your life. Recognize the purity and sincerity in the hearts that beat alongside yours. Do not wait for absence to reveal the depth of affection that surrounds you. Embrace it wholeheartedly, nurture it with care, and let gratitude guide your interactions. Sheetal's and my story stands as a testament to the transformative power of love, a love that transcends time and space, leaving an indelible mark on our souls. Though she may no longer walk beside me, her love endures, a gentle reminder to cherish each moment with those who matter most.

Let us learn from my journey, let us not wait for loss to teach us the value of true love. Instead, let us treasure and honour it every day, ensuring that our hearts remain open to receive and reciprocate the love that surrounds us. Sheetal, wherever you are, know that your love has forever changed me. In your absence, I vow to live with gratitude for the love we shared and to inspire others to embrace their true loves with open hearts and unyielding appreciation.

9 7 9 8 8 9 7 4 4 4 4 9 6